Meridian

By the same author

Revolutionary Petunias & Other Poems

Once

The Third Life of Grange Copeland

In Love & Trouble

Langston Hughes, American Poet

MERIDIAN

A Novel
By
Alice Walker

LANDMARK BOOKS

Santa Barbara, California
Oxford, England

First published 1976 in the United States by Harcourt Brace Jovanovich, Inc., and in Great Britain by The Women's Press, Limited.

Published in large print 1987 by arrangement with Harcourt Brace Jovanovich, Inc., and The Women's Press, Limited.

Library of Congress Cataloging-in-Publication Data
Walker, Alice, 1944–
Meridian.

1. Large type books. I. Title.
[PS3573.A425M4 1987] 813′.54 86-32189

ISBN 1-55736-019-7
10 9 8 7 6 5 4 3 2 1

ABC-Clio, Inc.
2040 Alameda Padre Serra
Santa Barbara, California 93103-1788

Clio Press Ltd.
55 St. Thomas Street
Oxford, OX1 1JG, England

This book is smyth-sewn and printed on acid-free paper ♾.
Manufactured in the United States of America.

For Staughton Lynd and Mary*am* L.
and for John Lewis the unsung

CONTENTS

I wish to thank the Radcliffe Institute, the MacDowell Colony and the Yaddo Corporation for their support during the writing of this book. I also thank Mel Leventhal and Rebecca Leventhal.

I did not know then how much was ended. When I look back now . . . I can still see the butchered women and children lying heaped and scattered all along the crooked gulch as plain as when I saw them with eyes still young. And I can see that something else died there in the bloody mud, and was buried in the blizzard. A people's dream died there. It was a beautiful dream . . . the nation's hoop is broken and scattered. There is no center any longer, and the sacred tree is dead.

—Black Elk, *Black Elk Speaks*

me•rid i•an, *n.* [L. *meridianus,* pertaining to midday, or to the south, from *meridies,* midday, the south; *medius,* middle and *dies,* day.]

1. the highest apparent point reached by a heavenly body in its course.

2. (a) the highest point of power, prosperity, splendor, etc.; zenith; apex; culmination; (b) the middle period of one's life, regarded as the highest point of health, vigor, etc.; prime.

3. noon. [*Obs.*]

4. in astronomy, an imaginary great circle of the celestial sphere passing through the poles of the heavens and the zenith and nadir of any given point, and cutting the equator at right angles.

5. in geography, (a) a great circle of the earth passing through the geographical poles and any given point on the earth's surface; (b) the half of such a circle between the poles; (c) any of the lines of longitude running north and south on a globe or map, representing such a circle or half-circle.

6. (a) a place or situation with its own distinctive character; (b) distinctive character.

7. a graduated ring of brass, in which a globe is suspended and revolves.

first meridian: see *prime meridian* under *prime.*

magnetic meridian: a carefully located meridian from which secondary or guide meridians may be constructed.

me•rid i•an, *a.*

1. of or at noon or, especially, of the position or power of the sun at noon.

2. of or passing through the highest point in the daily course of any heavenly body.
3. of or along a meridian.
4. of or at the highest point of prosperity, splendor, power, etc.
5. southern. [Rare.]

Meridian

The Last Return

Truman Held drove slowly into the small town of Chicokema as the two black men who worked at the station where he stopped for gas were breaking for lunch. They looked at him as he got out of his car and lifted their Coca-Colas in a slight salute. They were seated on two boxes in the garage, out of the sun, and talked in low, unhurried voices while Truman chewed on a candy bar and supervised the young white boy, who had come scowling out of the station office to fill up the car with gas. Truman had driven all night from New York City, and his green Volvo was covered with grease and dust; crushed insects blackened the silver slash across the grill.

"Know where I can get this thing washed?" he called, walking toward the garage.

"Sure do," one of the men said, and rose slowly, letting the last swallow of Coke leave the bottle into his mouth. He had just lifted a crooked forefinger to point when a small boy dressed in tattered jeans bounded up to him, the momentum of his flight almost knocking the older man down.

"Here, wait a minute," said the man, straightening up. "Where's the fire?"

"Ain't no fire," said the boy, breathlessly. "It's that woman in the cap. She's staring down the tank!"

"Goodness gracious," said the other man, who had been on the point of putting half a doughnut into his mouth. He and the other man wiped their hands quickly on their orange monkey suits and glanced at the clock over the garage. "We've got time," said the man with the doughnut.

"I reckon," said the other one.

"What's the matter?" asked Truman. "Where are you going?"

The boy who had brought the news had now somehow obtained the half-doughnut and was chewing it very fast, with one eye cocked on the soda that was left in one of the bottles.

"This town's got a big old army tank," he muttered, his mouth full, "and now they going to have to aim it on the woman in the cap, 'cause she act like she don't even know they got it."

He had swallowed the doughnut and also polished off the drink.

"Gotta go," he said, taking off after the two service station men who were already running around the corner out of sight.

The town of Chicokema did indeed own a tank. It had been bought during the sixties when the townspeople who were white felt under attack from "outside agitators"—those members of the black community who thought equal rights for all should extend to blacks. They had painted it white, decked it with ribbons (red, white, and of course blue) and parked it in the public square. Beside it was a statue of a Confederate soldier facing north whose right leg, while the tank was being parked, was permanently crushed.

The first thing Truman noticed was that although the streets around the square were lined with people, no one was saying anything. There was such a deep silence they did not even seem to be breathing; his own footsteps sounded loud on the sidewalk. Except for the unnatural quiet it was a square exactly like that in hundreds of small Southern towns. There was an expanse of patchy sunburned lawn surrounding a brick courthouse, a fringe of towering pine and magnolia trees, and concrete walks that were hot and clean, except for an occasional wad of discarded chewing gum that stuck to the bottoms of one's shoes.

On the side of the square where Truman now was, the stores were run-down, their signs advertising tobacco and Olde Milwaukee beer faded from too many years under a hot sun. Across the square the stores were better kept. There were newly dressed manikins behind sparkling glass panes and window boxes filled with red impatiens.

"What's happening?" he asked, walking up to an old man who was bent carefully and still as a bird over his wide broom.

"Well," said the sweeper, giving Truman a guarded look as he clutched his broom, supporting himself on it, "some of the children wanted to get in to see the dead lady, you know, the mummy woman, in the trailer over there, and our day for seeing her ain't till Thursday."

"*Your* day?"

"That's what I said."

"But the Civil Rights Movement changed all that!"

"I seen rights come and I seen 'em go," said the sweeper sullenly, as if daring Truman to disagree. "You're a stranger here or you'd know this is for the folks that work in that guano plant outside town. *Po'* folks.

"The people who don't have to work in that plant claim the folks that do smells so bad they can't stand to be in the same place with 'em. But you know what guano is made out of. Whew. You'd smell worse than a dead fish, too!"

"But you don't work there, do you?"

"Used to. Laid off for being too old."

Across the square to their left was a red and gold circus wagon that glittered in the sun. In tall, ornate gold letters over the side were the words, outlined in silver, "Marilene O'Shay, One of the Twelve Human Wonders of the World: Dead for Twenty-Five Years, Preserved in Life-Like Condition." Below this, a smaller legend was scrawled in red paint on four large stars: "Obedient Daughter," read one, "Devoted Wife," said another. The third was "Adoring Mother" and the fourth was "Gone Wrong." Over the fourth a vertical line of progressively flickering light bulbs moved continually downward like a perpetually cascading tear.

Truman laughed. "That's got to be a rip-off," he said.

"Course it is," said the sweeper, and spat. "But you know how childrens is, love to see anything that's weird."

The children were on the opposite side of the square from the circus wagon, the army tank partially blocking their view of it. They were dressed in black and yellow school uniforms and surrounded somebody or something like so many bees. Talking and gesticulating all at once, they raised a busy, humming sound.

The sweeper dug into his back pocket and produced a pink flier. He handed it to Truman to read. It was "The True Story of Marilene O'Shay."

According to the writer, Marilene's husband, Henry, Marilene had been an ideal woman, a "goddess," who had been given "everything she *thought* she wanted." She had owned a washing machine, furs, her own car and a full-time housekeeper-cook. All she had to do, wrote Henry, was "lay back and be pleasured." But she, "corrupted by the honeyed tongues of evildoers that dwell in high places far away," had gone outside the home to seek her "pleasuring," while still expecting him to foot the bills.

The oddest thing about her dried-up body, according to Henry's flier, and the one that—though it only reflected her sinfulness—bothered him most, was that its exposure to salt had caused it to darken. And, though he had attempted to paint her her original color from time to time, the paint always discolored. Viewers of her remains should be convinced of his wife's race, therefore, by the straightness and reddish color of her hair.

Truman returned the flier with a disgusted grunt. Across the square the children had begun to shuffle and dart about as if trying to get in line. Something about the composition of the group bothered him.

"They *are* all black," he said after a while, looking back at the sweeper. "Besides, they're too small to work in a plant."

"In the first place," said the sweeper, pointing, "there is some white kids in the bunch. They sort of overpowered by all the color. And in the second place, the folks who don't work in the guano plant don't draw the line at the mamas and papas, they throw in the childrens, too. Claim the smell of guano don't wash off.

"That mummy lady's husband, he got on the good side of the upper crust real quick: When the plant workers' children come round trying to get a peek at his old salty broad while some of *them* was over there, he called 'em dirty little bastards and shoo'em away. That's when this weird gal that strolled into town last year come in. She started to round up every one of the po' kids she could get her hands on. She look so burnt out and weird in that old cap she wear you'd think they'd be afraid of her—they too young to 'member when black folks marched a lot—but they not."

Catching his breath, Truman stood on tiptoe and squinted across the square. Standing with the children, directly opposite both the circus wagon and the tank, was Meridian, dressed in dungarees and wearing a light-colored, visored cap, of the sort worn by motormen on trains. On one side of them, along the line of bright stores, stood a growing crowd of white people. Along the shabby stores where Truman and the sweeper stood was a still-as-death crowd of blacks. A white woman flew out of the white crowd and snatched one of the white children, slapping the child's shoulders as she hustled it out of sight. With alarm, Truman glanced at the tank in the center of the square. At that moment, two men were crawling into it, and a phalanx of police, their rifles pointing upward, rushed to defend the circus wagon.

It was as if Meridian waited for them to get themselves nicely arranged. When the two were in the tank and swinging its muzzle in her direction, and the others were making a line across the front of the wagon, she raised her hand once and marched off the curb. The children fell into line behind her, their heads held high and their feet scraping the pavement.

"Now they will burst into song," muttered Truman, but they did not.

Meridian did not look to the right or to the left. She passed the people watching her as if she didn't know it was on her account they were there. As she approached the tank the blast of its engine starting sent a cloud of pigeons fluttering, with the sound of rapid, distant shelling, through the air, and the muzzle of the tank swung tantalizingly side to side—as if to tease her—before it settled directly toward her chest. As she drew nearer the tank, it seemed to grow larger and whiter than ever and she seemed smaller and blacker than ever. And then, when she reached the tank she stepped lightly, deliberately, right in front of it, rapped smartly on its carapace—as if knocking on a door—then raised her arm again. The children pressed onward, through the ranks of the arrayed riflemen and up to the circus car door. The silence, as Meridian kicked open the door, exploded in a mass exhalation of breaths, and the men who were in the tank crawled sheepishly out again to stare.

"God!" said Truman without thinking. "How can you not love somebody like that!"

"Because she thinks *she's* God," said the old sweeper, "or else she just ain't all there. *I* think she ain't all there, myself."

"What do you mean?" asked Truman.

"Listen," said the man, "as far as I'm concerned, this stuff she do don't make no sense. One of my buddies already done told me about this mummified white woman. He says she ain't nothing but a skeleton. She just got long hair that her ol' man claims is still growing. That fool sets up breshin' it every night." He snorted and sucked his two remaining side teeth.

"Just because he caught her giving some away, he shot the man, strangled the wife. Throwed'em both into Salt Lake. Explained everthing to the 'thorities up there and they forgive him, preacher forgive him, everybody forgive him. Even her ma.

'Cause this bitch was doing him wrong, and that ain't right!"

He poked Truman in the ribs. "That ain't right, is it?"

"No," said Truman, who was watching Meridian.

"Well sir, years later she washed up on shore, and he claimed he recognized her by her long red hair. He'd done forgive her by then and felt like he wouldn't mind having her with him again. Thought since she was so generous herself she wouldn't mind the notion of him sharing her with the Amurican public. He saw it was a way to make a little spare change in his ol' age."

Another poke in the ribs. A giggle.

"He drags her around from town to town, charging a quarter to see her. Course we don't have to pay but a dime, being po' and smelly and all. I wouldn't pay nothing to see her, myself. The hussy wasn't worth a dime."

The schoolchildren were passing in and out of the wagon. Some adult blacks had joined the line. Then some poor whites.

"Her casket though!" said the old sweeper. "They tell me it is great. One of those big jobs made of metal, with pink velvet upholstery and gold and silver handles. Cost upwards of a thousand dollars!"

The crowd, by now, had begun to disperse. The last of the children were leaving the wagon. Meridian stood at the bottom step, watching the children and the adults come down. She rested one foot on the rail that ran under the wagon and placed one hand in her pocket. Truman, who knew so well the features of her face, imagined her slightly frowning from the effort to stand erect and casually, just that way.

"Her name's Meridian," Truman said to the sweeper.

"You don't know her personally?" asked the sweeper in sympathy.

"Believe it or not," he said.

The door to Meridian's house was not locked, so Truman went in and walked around. In the room that contained her sleeping bag he paused to read her wallpaper—letters she had stuck up side by side, neatly, at eye level. The first contained Bible verses and was written by Meridian's mother, the gist of which was that Meridian had failed to honor not just her parents, but anyone. The others were signed "Anne-Marion" (whom Truman knew had been Meridian's friend and roommate in college) and were a litany of accusations, written with much viciousness and condescension. They all began: "Of course you are misguided . . ." and "Those, like yourself, who do not admit the truth . . ." and "You have never, being weak and insensitive to History, had any sense of priorities . . . ," etc. Why should Meridian have bothered to keep them? On some she had gamely scribbled: "Yes, yes. No. Some of the above. No, no. Yes. *All* of the above."

Above and below this strip of letters the walls were of decaying sheetrock, with uneven patches of dried glue as if the original wallpaper had been hastily removed. The sun through a tattered gray window shade cast the room in dim gray light, and as he glanced at the letters—walking slowly clockwise around the room—he had the feeling he was in a cell.

It was Meridian's house—the old sweeper had pointed it out to him—and this was Meridian's room. But he felt as if he were in a cell. He looked about for some means of making himself comfortable, but there was nothing. She owned no furniture, beyond the sleeping bag, which, on inspection, did not appear to be very clean. However, from his student days, working in the Movement in the South, he knew how pleasant it could be to nap on a shaded front porch. With a sigh of nostalgia and anticipation, Truman bent down to remove his hot city shoes.

"How was I to know it was you?" he asked, lying, when her eyes opened. He could not have walked up to her in front of all those people. He was embarrassed for her.

"Why, Che Guevara," she said dreamily, then blinked her eyes. "Truman?" He had popped up too often in her life for her to be surprised. "You look like Che Guevara. Not," she began, and caught her breath, "not by accident I'm sure." She was referring to his olive-brown skin, his black eyes, and the neatly trimmed beard and moustache he'd grown since the last time she saw him. He was also wearing a tan cotton jacket of the type worn by Chairman Mao.

"You look like a revolutionary," she said. "Are you?"

"Only if all artists are. I'm still painting, yes." And he scrutinized her face, her bones, which he had painted many times.

"What are you continuing to do to yourself?" he asked, holding her bony, ice-cold hand in his. Her face alarmed him. It was wasted and rough, the skin a sallow, unhealthy brown, with pimples across her forehead and on her chin. Her eyes were glassy and yellow and did not seem to focus at once. Her breath, like her clothes, was sour.

Four men had brought her home, hoisted across their shoulders exactly as they would carry a coffin, her eyes closed, barely breathing, arms folded across her chest, legs straight. They had passed him without speaking as he lay, attempting to nap, on the porch, placed her on her sleeping bag, and left. They had not even removed her cap, and while she was still unconscious Truman had pushed back her cap as he wiped her face with his moistened handkerchief and saw she had practically no hair.

"Did they hurt you out there?" he asked.

"They didn't touch me," she said.

"You're just sick then?"

"Of course I'm sick," snapped Meridian. "Why else would I spend all this time trying to get well!"

"You have a strange way of trying to get well!"

But her voice became softer immediately, as she changed the subject.

"You look just *like* Che," she said, "while I must look like death eating a soda cracker." She reached up and pulled at the sides of her cap, bringing the visor lower over her eyes. Just before she woke up she had been dreaming about her father; they were running up and down steep green hills chasing each other. She'd been yelling "Wait!" and "Stop!" at the top of her lungs, but when she heard him call the same words to her she speeded up. Neither of them waited or stopped. She was exhausted and so she had woke up.

"I was waiting for you to come home—lying out on the porch—when I saw these people coming carrying a body"—Truman smiled—"which turned out to be you. They carried you straight as a board across their shoulders. How'd they do that?"

Meridian shrugged. "They're used to carrying corpses."

"Ever since I've been here people have been bringing boxes and boxes of food. Your house is packed with stuff to eat. One man even brought a cow. The first thing that cow did was drop cowshit all over the front walk. Whew," said Truman, squeezing her hand, "folks sure are something down here."

"They're grateful people," said Meridian. "They *appreciate* it when someone volunteers to suffer."

"Well, you can't blame them for not wanting to go up against a tank. After all, everybody isn't bulletproof, like you."

"We have an understanding," she said.

"Which is?"

"That if somebody has to go it might as well be the person who's ready."

"And are you ready?"

"Now? No. What you see before you is a woman in the process of changing her mind."

"That's hard to believe."

"It's amazing how little that matters."

"You mean that kindly, of course."

"Yes."

"Tell me," said Truman, who did not want to show how sad he suddenly felt, "did you look inside the wagon yourself?"

"No."

"Why not?"

"I knew that whatever the man was selling was irrelevant to me, useless."

"The whole thing was useless, if you ask me," said Truman, with bitterness. "You make yourself a catatonic behind a lot of meaningless action that will never get anybody anywhere. What good did it do those kids to see that freak's freaky wife?"

"She was a fake. They discovered that. There was no salt, they said, left in the crevices of her eyesockets or in her hair. This town is near the ocean, you know, the children have often seen dead things wash up from the sea. They said she was made of plastic and were glad they hadn't waited till Thursday when they would have to pay money to see her. Besides, it was a hot day. They were bored. There was nothing else to do."

"Did you fall down in front of them?"

"I try never to do that. I never have. Some of the men—the ones who brought me home—followed me away from the square; they always follow me home after I perform, in case I need them. I fell down only when I was out of the children's sight."

"And they folded your arms?"

"They folded my arms."

"And straightened your legs."

"They're very gentle and good at it."

"Do they know why you fall down?"

"It doesn't bother them. They have a saying for people who fall down as I do: If a person is hit hard enough, even if she stands, she falls. Don't you think that's perceptive?"

"I don't know what to think. I never have. Do you have a doctor?"

"I don't need one. I am getting much better by myself. . . ." Meridian moved her fingers, then lifted her arms slightly off the floor. "See, the paralysis is going away already." She continued to raise and lower her arms, flexing her fingers and toes as she did so. She rolled her shoulders forward and up and raised and twisted her ankles. Each small movement made her face look happier, even as the effort exhausted her.

Truman watched her struggle to regain the use of her body. "I grieve in a different way," he said.

"I know," Meridian panted.

"What do you know?"

"I know you grieve by running away. By pretending you were never there."

"When things are finished it is best to leave."

"And pretend they were never started?"

"Yes."

"But that's not possible."

Meridian had learned this in New York, nearly ten summers ago.

"You are a coward," one of the girls said then, though they knew she was not a coward.

"A masochist," sniffed another.

And Meridian had sat among them on the floor, her hands clasping the insides of her sneakers, her head down. To join this group she must make a declaration of her willingness to die for the Revolution, which she had done. She must also answer the question "Will you kill for the Revolution?" with a positive Yes. This, however, her tongue could not manage. Through her mind was running a small voice that screamed: "Something's missing in me. Something's *missing!*" And the voice made her heart pound and her ears roar. "Something the old folks with their hymns and proverbs forgot to put in! What is it? What? *What?*"

"Why don't you say something?" Anne-Marion's voice, angry and with the undisguised urgency of her contempt, attempted to suppress any tone of compassion. Anne-Marion had said, "Yes, I will kill for the Revolution" without a stammer; yet Meridian knew her tenderness, a vegetarian because she loved the eyes of cows.

Meridian alone was holding on to something the others had let go. If not completely, then partially—by their words today, their deeds tomorrow. But what none of them seemed to understand was that she felt herself to be, not holding on to something from the past, but *held* by something in the past: by the memory of old black men in the South who, caught by surprise in the eye of a camera, never shifted their position but looked directly back; by the sight of young girls singing in a country choir, their hair shining with brushings and grease, their voices the voices of angels. When she was transformed in church it was always by the purity of the singers' souls, which she could actually *hear,* the purity that lifted their songs like a flight of doves above her music-drunken head. If they committed murder—and to her even revolutionary murder was murder—*what would the music be like?*

She had once jokingly asked Anne-Marion to imagine the Mafia as a singing group. The Mafia, Anne-Marion had hissed, is not a revolutionary cadre!

"You hate yourself instead of hating them," someone said.

"Why don't you say something?" said another, jabbing her in the ribs.

This group might or might not do something revolutionary. It was after all a group of students, of intellectuals, converted to a belief in violence only after witnessing the extreme violence, against black dissidents, of the federal government and police. Would they rob a bank? Bomb a landmark? Blow up a police station? Would they ever be face to face with the enemy, guns drawn? Perhaps. Perhaps not. "But that isn't the point!" the small voice screeched. The point was, she could not think lightly of shedding blood. And the question of killing did not impress her as rhetorical at all.

They were waiting for her to speak. But what

could she say? Saying nothing, she remembered her mother and the day she lost her. She was thirteen, sitting next to her mother in church, drunk as usual with the wonderful music, the voices themselves almost making the words of songs meaningless; the girls, the women, the stalwart fathers singing

The day is past and gone
The evening shade appear
Oh may we all remember well
The night of death draw near

Sniffling, her heart breaking with love, it was her father's voice, discerned in clarity from all the others, that she heard. It enveloped her in an anguish for that part of him that was herself—how could he be so resigned to death, she thought. But how sweet his voice! It was her mother, however, whom she heeded, while trying not to: "Say it now, Meridian, and be saved. All He asks is that we acknowledge Him as our Master. Say you believe in Him." Looking at her daughter's tears: "Don't go against your heart!" But she had sat mute, watching her friends walking past her bench, accepting Christ, acknowledging God as their Master, Jesus their Savior, and her heart fluttered like that of a small bird about to be stoned. It was her father's voice that moved her, that voice that could come only from the life he lived. A life of withdrawal from the world, a life of constant awareness of death. It was the music that made her so tractable and willing she might have said anything, acknowledged anything, simply for peace from this pain that was rendered so exquisitely beautiful by the singers' voices.

But for all that her father sang beautifully, heartbreakingly, of God, she sensed he did not believe in Him in quite the same way her mother did. Her mind struck on a perennial conversation between her parents regarding the Indians:

"The Indians were living right here, in Georgia," said her father, "they had a town, an alphabet, a newspaper. They were going about their business, enjoying life . . . It was the same with them all over the country, and in Mexico, South America . . . doesn't this say anything to you?"

"No," her mother would say.

"And the women had babies and made pottery. And the men sewed moccasins and made drums out of hides and hollow logs."

"So?"

"It was a life, ruled by its own spirits."

"That's what you claim, anyway."

"And where is it now?"

Her mother sighed, fanning herself with a fan from the funeral home. "I never worry myself about those things. There's such a thing as progress. I didn't invent it, but I'm not going to argue with it either. As far as I'm concerned those people and how they kept off mosquitoes hasn't got a thing to do with me."

Meridian's mother would take up a fistful of wire clothes hangers, straighten them out, and red, yellow and white crepe paper and her shears, and begin to cut out rose petals. With a dull knife she scraped each petal against her thumb and then pressed both thumbs against the center of the petal to make a cup. Then she put smaller petals inside larger ones, made the bud of the rose by covering a small bail of aluminum foil with bright green paper, tied the completed flower head to the end of the clothes hanger, and stood the finished product in a churn already crowded with the artificial blooms. In winter she made small pillows, puckered and dainty, of many different colors. She stuck them in plastic bags that piled up in the closet. Prayer pillows, she called them. But they were too small for kneeling. They would only fit one knee, which Meridian's mother never seemed to notice.

Still, it is death not to love one's mother. Or so it seemed to Meridian, and so, understanding her mother as a willing know-nothing, a woman of ignorance and—in her ignorance—of cruelty, she loved her more than anything. But she respected even more her father's intelligence, though it seemed he sang, beautifully, only of death.

She struggled to retain her mother's hand, covering it with her own, and attempted to bring it to her lips. But her mother moved away, tears of anger and sadness coursing down her face. Her mother's love was gone, withdrawn, and there were conditions to be met before it would be returned. Conditions Meridian was never able to meet.

"Fallen asleep, have you?" It was a voice from the revolutionary group, calling her from a decidedly unrevolutionary past. They made her ashamed of that past, and yet all of them had shared it. The church, the music, the tolerance shown to different beliefs outside the community, the tolerance shown to strangers. She felt she loved them. But love was not what they wanted, it was not what they needed.

They needed her to kill. To say she would kill. She thought perhaps she could do it. Perhaps.

"I don't *know* if I can kill anyone . . ."

There was a relaxing of everyone. "Ah . . ."

"If I had to do it, perhaps I could. I would defend myself . . ."

"Sure you would . . ." sighed Anne-Marion, reining in the hatred about to run wild against her friend.

"Maybe I could sort of grow into the idea of killing other human beings . . ."

"Enemies . . ."

"Pigs . . ."

"But I'm not *sure* . . ."

"Oh, what a drag this girl is . . ."

"I know I want what is best for black people . . ."

"That's what we all want!"

"I know there must be a revolution . . ."

"Damn straight!"

"I know violence *is* as American as cherry pie!"

"Rap on!"

"I know nonviolence has failed . . ."

"Then you will kill for the Revolution, not just die for it?" Anne-Marion's once lovely voice, beloved voice. "Like a fool!" the voice added, bitterly and hard.

"I don't know."

"Shee-it . . . !"

"But can you *say* you probably will? That you *will*."

"No."

Everyone turned away.

"What will you do? Where will you go?" Only Anne-Marion still cared enough to ask, though her true eyes—with their bright twinkle—had been replaced with black marbles.

"I'll go back to the people, live among them, like Civil Rights workers used to do."

"You're not serious?"

"Yes," she had said, "I am serious."

And so she had left the North and come back South, moving from one small town to another, finding jobs—some better or worse than others—to support herself; remaining close to the people—to see them, to be with them, to understand them and herself, the people who now fed her and tolerated her and also, in a fashion, cared about her.

Each time Truman visited Meridian he found her with less and less furniture, fewer and fewer pieces of clothing, less of a social position in the community—wherever it was—where she lived. From being a teacher who published small broadsides of poems, she had hired herself out as a gardener, as a waitress at middle-class black parties, and had occasionally worked as a dishwasher and cook.

"And now you're here," said Truman, indicating the bareness of the room.

"*Vraiment*," said Meridian, and smiled at the startled look on Truman's face. "Why, you've forgotten your French!" she said. And then, soberly, "We really must let each other go, you know."

"You mean I really must let *you* go," said Truman. "You cut me loose a long time ago."

"And how is Lynne?"

"I haven't seen her in a long time. I've only seen her a few times since Camara died."

"I liked your daughter."

"She was beautiful." And then, because he did not want to talk about his daughter or his wife, he said, "I've never understood your illness, the paralysis, the breaking down . . . the way you can face a tank with absolute calm one minute and the next be unable to move. I always think of you as so strong, but look at you!"

"I *am* strong, actually," said Meridian, cockily, for someone who looked near death and had to do exercises before her body allowed her to crawl or stand. "I'm just not Superwoman."

"And why can't Anne-Marion leave you alone?" asked Truman, nodding at the letters on the wall. "Anyone who could write such hateful things is a real bitch."

"To tell the truth," said Meridian, "I keep the letters because they contain the bitch's handwriting."

"You're kidding?" asked Truman.

"No, I'm not," said Meridian.

MEDGAR EVERS/JOHN F. KENNEDY/ MALCOLM X/MARTIN LUTHER KING/ ROBERT KENNEDY/CHE GUEVARA/ PATRICE LAMUMBA/GEORGE JACKSON/ CYNTHIA WESLEY/ADDIE MAE COLLINS/ DENISE MCNAIR/CAROLE ROBERTSON/ VIOLA LIUZZO

It was a decade marked by death. Violent and inevitable. Funerals became engraved on the brain, intensifying the ephemeral nature of life. For many in the South it was a decade reminiscent of earlier times, when oak trees sighed over their burdens in the wind; Spanish moss draggled bloody to the ground; amen corners creaked with grief; and the thrill of being able, once again, to endure unendurable loss produced so profound an ecstasy in mourners that they strutted, without noticing their feet, along the thin backs of benches: their piercing shouts of anguish and joy never interrupted by an inglorious fall. They shared rituals for the dead to be remembered.

But now television became the repository of memory, and each onlooker grieved alone.

It was during the first televised Kennedy funeral that Anne-Marion Coles became quite conscious of Meridian Hill. She had seen her around the campus before, but never really to speak to. Meridian appeared so aloof she could sit at a table for four in the dining room and never be asked to share it; or, if she were asked, the question would be put timidly, with deference. This barrier she erected seemed to astonish her, and when finally approached—whether in the dining room, the chapel, or under the campus trees—she was likely to seem too eager in her response, too generous, too friendly, her dark face whipped quickly into liveliness, and dark, rather sad eyes crinkled brightly into gladness.

Anne-Marion had the audacity of the self-confident person who, against whatever odds, intends to succeed. Hers was an exploitative rather than an altruistic nature, and she would never have attempted penetrating Meridian's reserve if she had not sensed behind it an intriguing and valuable inner life—an exploration of which would enrich her own existence. That she would learn to care for Meridian she did not foresee.

She sat across from Meridian as she and the other honor students watched the Kennedy family stride off toward Arlington National Cemetery behind the shattered body of their dead John. Jackie Kennedy, it was suggested by a newsman, had been given something that helped her not to cry. The students had been given nothing, and so they cried small floods. Meridian's face, grayish-blue from the television light, glistened with tears that dripped off her chin onto her blue cotton shirt. Slumped forward with grief, she did not bother to raise her hands from her lap, where they lay palms up, empty. She shivered as if she were cold.

Earlier that same year, when Medgar Evers was assassinated, Meridian had planted a wild sweet shrub bush among the plants in the formal garden in front of the honors house. Each day the jealous gardener had pulled a bit more of its delicate roots to the surface, so that it too soon died. Remembering this, seeing her shiver, Anne-Marion held out her sweater to Meridian. Scarcely looking at her, Meridian took it and wrapped herself up tight.

The Wild Child

The Wild Child was a young girl who had managed to live without parents, relatives or friends for all of her thirteen years. It was assumed she was thirteen, though no one knew for sure. She did not know herself, and even if she had known, she was not capable of telling. Wile Chile, as the people in the neighborhood called her (saying it slowly, musically, so that it became a kind of lewd, suggestive song), had appeared one day in the slum that surrounded Saxon College when she was already five or six years old. At that time, there were two of them, Wile Chile and a smaller boy. The boy soon disappeared. It was rumored that he was stolen by the local hospital for use in experiments, but this was never looked into. In any case, Wile Chile was seen going through garbage cans and dragging off pieces of discarded furniture, her ashy black arms straining at the task. When a neighbor came out of her house to speak to her, Wile Chile bolted, not to be seen again for several weeks. This was the pattern she followed for years. She would be seen scavenging for food in the garbage cans, and when called to, she would run.

In summer she wore whatever was available in castoff shorts and cotton tops. Or she would wear a pair of large rayon panties, pulled up under her arms, and nothing else. In winter she put together a collection of wearable junk and topped it with a mangy fur jacket that came nearly to the ground. By the age of eight (by the neighbors' reckoning) she had begun to smoke, and, as she dug about in the debris, kicking objects this way and that (and cursing, the only language she knew), she puffed on cigarette butts with a mature and practiced hand.

It was four or five winters after they first spotted her that the neighbors noticed Wile Chile was pregnant. They were critical of the anonymous "low-down dirty dog" who had done the impregnating, but could not imagine what to do. Wile Chile rummaged about as before, eating rancid food, dressing herself in castoffs, cursing and bolting, and smoking her brown cigarettes.

It was while she was canvassing voters in the neighborhood that Meridian first heard of The Wild Child. The neighbors had by then tried to capture her: A home for her lying-in had been offered. They failed to catch her, however. As one neighbor explained it, Wile Chile was slipperier than a greased pig, and unfortunately the comparison did not end there. Her odor was said to be formidable. The day Meridian saw The Wild Child she withdrew to her room in the honors house for a long time. When the other students looked into her room they were surprised to see her lying like a corpse on the floor beside her bed, eyes closed and hands limp at her sides. While lying there she did not respond to anything; not the call to lunch, not the phone, nothing. On the second morning the other students were anxious, but on that morning she was up.

With bits of cake and colored beads and unblemished cigarettes she tempted Wile Chile and finally captured her. She brought her onto the campus with a catgut string around her arm; when Wile Chile tried to run Meridian pulled her back. Into a tub went Wile Chile, whose body was caked with mud and rust, whose hair was matted with dust, and whose loud obscenities mocked Meridian's soothing voice. Wile Chile shouted words that were never uttered in the honors house. Meridian, splattered with soap and mud, broke down and laughed.

At dinner Wile Chile upset her tablemates with the uncouthness of her manners. Ignoring their horrified stares she drank from the tea pitcher and put cigarette ashes in her cup. She farted, as if to music, raising a thigh.

The house mother, called upon in desperation by the other honor students, attempted to persuade Meridian that The Wild Child was not her responsibility.

"She must not stay here," she said gravely. "Think of the influence. This is a school for young ladies." The house mother's marcel waves shone like real sea waves, and her light-brown skin was pearly under a mask of powder. Wile Chile trembled to see her and stood cowering in a corner.

The next morning, while Meridian phoned schools for special children and then homes for unwed mothers—only to find there were none that would accept Wile Chile—The Wild Child escaped. Running heavily across a street, her stomach the largest part of her, she was hit by a speeder and killed.

Sojourner

Meridian lived in a small corner room high under the eaves of the honors house and had decorated the ceiling, walls, backs of doors and the adjoining toilet with large photographs of trees and rocks and tall hills and floating clouds, which she claimed she *knew.*

While Meridian was thin and seemed to contain the essence of silence (so that hearing her laugh was always a surprise), her new friend, Anne-Marion, was rounded and lush, brash and eager to argue over the smallest issues. Her temper was easily lost. When she was attempting to be nonviolent and a policeman shoved her, she dug her nails into her arms to restrain herself, but could never resist sticking out, to its full extent, her energetic and expressive pink tongue.

"Meridian," she would whisper through clenched teeth, "tell me something sad or funny, *quick*, before I kick this bastard in the balls."

Anne-Marion was entirely unsympathetic to daily chapel, notoriously unresponsive to preachers —though she once declared she would follow King and "that handsome Andy Young" through the deepest dark swamp—and had no intention of singing or praying in public. If she bowed her head during protest demonstrations it was to see if her shoelace had come untied, and if she sang it was a song muttered through clenched teeth. She did not see why anyone should worry about her soul, even the people she marched with. "When it gives me trouble," she'd sneer, "I'll call y'all." In this, she and Meridian were exactly alike, except if some pathetic, distracted old marcher wished to bend Meridian's ear about his or her Jesus, Meridian would stand patiently and listen. She was constantly wanting to know about the songs: "Where did such and such a one come from?" or "How many years do you think black people have been singing this?"

Anne-Marion had also taken the first opportunity—once she had actually seen a natural on another woman's head—to cut off all her hair. For this she was called before the Dean of Women (whom she promptly christened "the Dead of Women")—whose own hair was long, processed and lavender—and reprimanded.

"First blue jeans before six o'clock and now this!" said the Dead of Women. "It is becoming clear you are some kind of oddity."

"Under the circumstances," Anne-Marion told Meridian later, "hearing this from her was a relief!"

Meridian agreed. A future of processed lavender hair didn't amount to much.

Like Meridian, Anne-Marion was a deviate in the honors house: there because of her brilliance but only tolerated because it was clear she was one, too, on whom true Ladyhood would never be conferred. Most of the students—timid, imitative, bright enough but never daring, were being ushered nearer to Ladyhood every day. It was for this that their parents had sent them to Saxon College. They learned to make French food, English tea and German music without once having the urge to slip off the heavily guarded campus at five in the morning to photograph a strange tree as the light hit it just the right way—as Meridian had—or to risk being raped in a rough neighborhood as they attempted to discover the economic causes of inner-city crime, as had Anne-Marion.

Meridian and Anne-Marion walked together, as they had many times before. Only now they moved slowly, carefully, their dark dresses down to the tops of their polished shoes, and their hands, underneath the narrow coffin, nearly touched. The mourners in front of them stopped, and a few stepped out of the line to stare at what appeared to be a commotion at the gate.

"I never would have guessed Wile Chile had so many friends," said Meridian dryly. Even in her heavy black dress and thick braided hair Meridian weighed less than a hundred pounds, and her deep-brown skin was filmed slightly with perspiration that reddened it. When she was thoughtful or when she was unaware of being observed, her face seemed deeply sad, as if she knew there was no hope, in the long run, for anyone in the world, and that whatever she was doing at the time was destined for a short, if perfect, life. When she smiled, as she did often when talking to her friends, this look of anticipated doom was almost wiped away, though traces of it always lingered in the depths of her eyes.

She was never thought of as a *pretty* girl. People might say she looked interesting, mysterious, older than her years and therefore intriguing, but she was considered *approaching beautiful* only when she looked sad. When she laughed, this beauty broke; and people, captivated by the sad quality of her face, seemed compelled to joke with her just long enough to cause her to laugh and lose it. Then, freed from their interest in her, they walked away. After these encounters, her mouth still quivering and contracting from her laughter of a moment before, she would curl her toes and stand on one foot, leaning like a crane into the space around her, rocked by the thump-thump of her bewildered—and, she felt then, rather stupid—heart.

Anne-Marion, seeing this happen too frequently to Meridian without anything being learned from it, always felt the urge, at the point where Meridian leaned on one foot, to rush forward and kick her.

Now Meridian strained upward on her toes in an effort to improve her view, but could see nothing beyond the milling about of the people at the gate.

"That flaky bastard," said Anne-Marion, her dark eyes flashing. "That mother's scum is going to turn us around."

"He wouldn't," said Meridian mildly.

"You wait and see. He's scared of us causing a commotion that could get in the cracker papers, just when he's fooled'em that Saxon Knee-grows are *finally* your ideal improved type."

Anne-Marion wiped her brow and heaved the coffin more firmly against her cheek.

"He ain't nothing but a dishrag for those crackers downtown. He can't stand up to'em no more than piss can fall upward. His mama should've drowned him in the commode the minute he was born."

"Leave folks' mamas alone," said Meridian, although Anne-Marion made her smile. She was relieved that the line had begun, slowly, to move again. Wile Chile was getting heavier with each pause. Soon they were abreast of the guards at the gate. "Hey, brother," she called to the good-looking one.

"Y'all gon' run into trouble," he called back nonchalantly.

It still surprised her to see a black man wearing a uniform and holstered gun. What was he protecting? she wondered. If he was protecting the campus, how silly that was, because nobody would ever dare harm the lovely old campus buildings; and he couldn't be protecting the students, because they were only just now coming onto the campus, following the six young women who sweated under the casket (which they had paid for) that held The Wild Child's body; and he couldn't be afraid of the crowd of Wile Chile's neighbors, whose odors and groans and hymns drifted up to them pungent with poverty and despair. Humbly, they were bringing up the rear.

Anne-Marion, having given up on winning over the guards long ago, refused now even to look at them. She could not see policemen, guards and such. "I have uniform blindness," she explained.

The street outside the gate was ordinary enough, with patched potholes and a new signal light just in front of the gate. The fence that surrounded the campus was hardly noticeable from the street and appeared, from the outside, to be more of an attempt at ornamentation than an effort to contain or exclude. Only the students who lived on campus learned, often painfully, that the beauty of a fence is no guarantee that it will not keep one penned in as securely as one that is ugly.

A dampness peculiar to the climate was turned lightly warm by the clear sunshine, and blossoms on apple and pear and cherry trees lifted the skeptical eye in wonder and peace. Running through so much green the road was as white as an egg, as if freshly scrubbed, and the red brick buildings, older than anyone still alive, sparkled in the sun.

"I'd like to wreck this place," Anne-Marion said, unmoved.

"You'd have to wreck me first," said Meridian. She needed this clean, if artificial, air to breathe.

There was, in the center of the campus, the largest magnolia tree in the country. It was called The Sojourner. Classes were sometimes held in it; a podium and platform had been built into its lower branches, with wooden steps leading up to them. The Sojourner had been planted by a slave on the Saxon plantation—later, of course, Saxon College. The slave's name was Louvinie. Louvinie was tall, thin, strong and not very pleasant to look at. She had a chin that stuck out farther than it should and she wore black headrags that made a shelf over her eyebrows. She became something of a local phenomenon in plantation society because it was believed she *could not* smile. In fact, throughout her long lifetime nothing even resembling a smile ever came to her poked-out lips.

In her own country in West Africa she had been raised in a family whose sole responsibility was the weaving of intricate tales with which to entrap people who hoped to get away with murder. This is how it worked: Her mother and father would be visited by the elders of the village, who walked the two miles to their hut singing the solemnest songs imaginable in order to move her parents' hearts, and to make it easier for the spirits who hung around the hut to help them in their trouble. The elders would tell of some crime done in the village by a person or persons unknown. Louvinie's parents would ask a few questions: How was the person murdered? What was stolen, other than the life? Where were the other villagers at the time? etc., all the while making marks on the floor of the hut with two painted sticks. The sticks had no meaning except as a distraction: Louvinie's parents did not like to be stared at.

When the elders left, Louvinie's mother would

change her face with paint and cover up her hair and put on a new dress and take up residence in the village proper. In a few days she would come back, and she and her husband would begin to make up a story to fit the activities of the criminal. When they completed it, they presented it to the villagers, who congregated in the dead of night to listen. Each person listening was required to hold a piece of treated fiber plant under his or her arm, snugly into the armpit. At the end of the story these balls of fiber were collected, and from them Louvinie's parents were able to identify the guilty party. How they were able to do this they had never had the chance to teach her.

On the Saxon plantation in America Louvinie had been placed in charge of the kitchen garden. She was considered too ugly to work in the house, and much too dour to be around the children. The children, however, adored her. When pressed, she would tell them stories of blood-curdling horror. They followed her wherever she went and begged her to tell them all the scary, horrible stories that she knew. She was pleased to do so, and would tell stories that made their hair stand on end. She made up new, American stories when the ones she remembered from Africa had begun to bore.

She might have continued telling stories had there not occurred a tragedy in the Saxon household that came about through no real fault of her own. It had never been explained to her that the youngest of the Saxon children, an only son, suffered from an abnormally small and flimsy heart.

Encouraged by the children to become more and more extravagant in her description, more pitiless in her plot, Louvinie created a masterpiece of fright, and, bursting with the delight she always felt when creating (but never smiling at all—which seemed curious, even to the children), she sat under a tree at the back of the garden just as the sun was sinking slowly through a black cloud bank in the west, and told the children the intricate, chilling story of the old man whose hobby was catching and burying children up to their necks and then draping their heads—which stuck up in rows, like cabbages—with wriggly eels dipped in honey. Long before the culprit received his comeuppance, young Saxon had slumped dead to the ground of a heart attack. He was seven years old.

Many, many years ago, on the banks of the Lalocac River, in deepest Africa, there lived a man blacker than the night, whose occupation was catching little white children—those who had lost at least one tooth to the snags of time—and planting them in his garden. He buried everything except their heads: These he left above ground because he liked to hear them wail and scream and call for their mothers, who, of course, did not know where they were and never came.

He fed them honey and live eels still wriggling that slipped through their lips and down their throats while underneath their ears the eels' tails still struggled and slid. At night the children's heads were used as warming posts for the man's pet snakes, all of them healthy and fat and cold as ice, and loving to flick a keen, quick tail into a snuffling, defenseless nose. . . . The man used to laugh as he—

This portion of Louvinie's story was later discovered on a yellowed fragment of paper and was kept under glass in the Saxon library. It was in the childish handwriting of one of the older Saxon girls.

Louvinie's tongue was clipped out at the root. Choking on blood, she saw her tongue ground under the heel of Master Saxon. Mutely, she pleaded for it, because she knew the curse of her native land: Without one's tongue in one's mouth or in a special spot of one's own choosing, the singer in one's soul was lost forever, to grunt and snort through eternity like a pig.

Louvinie's tongue was kicked toward her in a hail of sand. It was like a thick pink rose petal, bloody at the root. In her own cabin she smoked it until it was as soft and pliable as leather. On a certain day, when the sun turned briefly black, she buried it under a scrawny magnolia tree on the Saxon plantation.

Even before her death forty years later the tree had outgrown all the others around it. Other slaves believed it possessed magic. They claimed the tree could talk, make music, was sacred to birds and possessed the power to obscure vision. Once in its branches, a hiding slave could not be seen.

In Meridian's second year at Saxon there was talk of cutting down the tree, and she had joined members of the Chamber Music Ensemble and their dotty Hungarian conductor when they chained themselves to its trunk. They had long ago dubbed The Sojourner "The Music Tree," and would not stand to have it cut down, not even for a spanking new music building that a Northern philanthropist—unmindful that his buildings had already eaten up most of Saxon's precious greenness—was eager to give. The tree was spared, but the platform and podium were dismantled, and the lower branches and steps—which had made access to the upper reaches of the tree so delightfully easy—were trimmed away. And why? Because students—believing the slaves of a hundred and fifty years ago—used the platform and who knows, even the podium, as places to make love. Meridian had made something approaching love there herself. And it was true, she had not been seen.

So many tales and legends had grown up around The Sojourner that students of every persuasion had a choice of which to accept. There was only one Sojourner ceremony, however, that united all the students at Saxon—the rich and the poor, the very black-skinned (few though they were) with the very fair, the stupid and the bright—and that was the Commemoration of Fast Mary of the Tower.

It was related that during the twenties a young girl named Mary had had a baby in the tower off one end of Tower Hall. She had concealed her pregnancy and muffled her cries (and of course was too ashamed to ask for help or tell anybody anything) as the child was being born. Then she had carefully chopped the infant into bits and fed it into the commode. The bits stuck and Fast Mary was caught. Caught, she was flogged before her instructors and her parents. At home she was locked in her room and denied the presence of a window. She hanged herself after three months.

Any girl who had ever prayed for her period to come was welcome to the commemoration, which was held in the guise of a slow May Day dance around the foot of The Sojourner (which had been, it was said, Fast Mary's only comfort and friend on Saxon campus). It was the only time in all the many social activities at Saxon that every girl was considered equal. On that day, they held each other's hands tightly.

The tree was visible from outside the campus walls, but its true magnificence was apparent only after one got near enough for a closer look, though then it was like staring into the side of a tall, rather lumpy building. From the road near the gate the mourners behind Wile Chile's body could see the top, and the massive body and foliage of the tree, in full bloom, was like a huge mountain lit with candles. Across from the square that held the tree, on both sides, stood the empty red brick dormitories. Some windows were bedecked with flowers. Others were crammed with symbols of the campus sororities: QEZ or ZEQ, or whatever they were. Still others had large handpainted signs addressed to The Wild Child. "God Will Bless You, W.C." "We Love You, 'Wile Chile.'" "Tell God We Ready, Wild One." Other windows were simply empty or from them floated crepe paper streamers of purple and gold. These were the school colors.

Now the commotion at the front of the line, which had been going on for some time, reached them. The girl in front of them, whose name was Charlene, turned around. She was tall, heavily made up, and wore a reddish wig. Her accent reflected the St. Louis that she loved. She was a prisoner, temporarily, of the freshman class, a scholar under duress.

"They say the president say she can't have her funeral in you all's chapel." Charlene claimed nothing of the school except the men who walked over the grounds. She was chewing gum, popping it as she spoke.

Meridian laughed in spite of the occasion. She imagined the president—a tan, impeccably tailored patriarch with glinting, shifty gray eyes—coming up to The Wild Child's casket and saying, as if addressing a congregation: "We are sorry, young woman, but it is against the rules and regulations of this institution to allow you to conduct your funeral inside this chapel, which, as you may know, was donated to us by one of the finest robber baron families of New York. Besides, it is nearly time for Vespers, and you should have arranged for this affair *through the proper channels* much earlier."

And it seemed that, in fact, this was about what he did say, for there was a moiling about in front of the chapel (a stained-glass fortress made of stone, with gigantic circular columns supporting a jutting porch roof) as the mourners tried to plan what to do next.

When Meridian and Anne-Marion arrived at the chapel steps they found the two guards from the gate. The president, having issued his orders, had retired to his Victorian mansion on the hill, and they imagined him peering down at them from behind his Irish lace curtains on the second floor.

"I told y'all, y'all'd have trouble," said the guard. Only now he was not nonchalant. The mood of the students had changed from mournfnl to indignant. But they were nicely brought-up girls and their wrath was slow to rise. Still, it is the nature of wrath to rise, and the guard was no dope.

Anne-Marion, after the casket was lowered to the steps, examined the three-inch lock on the chapel door and looked about for a log or even a large rock to bash it in. But there was nothing. The people from the community, Wile Chile's neighbors, resplendent though they had felt themselves to be on entering Saxon gate—for they were in their Sunday-best outfits of red and yellow and peacock blue—now shrunk down inside their clothes and would not look the students in the eye. They appeared to melt away, slinking farther and farther back until they had vanished, like a snail that has salt poured on its tail. Holding out her arms and pleading, Meridian ran after them, but they would not come back.

The casket rested on the chapel steps, its color an orange to compete with the sunrise. There was a long moment of silence. Then the knowledge that The Wild Child was refused admittance to the chapel caused a cry to rise from the collective throats of the crowd in one long wail. For five minutes the air rang with shouts and the polite curses of young ladies whose home away from home the college was. They were so ashamed and angry they began to boo and stamp their feet and stick out their tongues through their tears. In the heat of their emotion they began to take off their jewelry and fling it to the ground—the heavy three-strand cultured pearl necklaces and the massive, circular gold-plated chastity pins, the globular, clustered earrings and their glittering bracelets of many-colored stones. They shook loose their straightened hair, and all the while they glared at the locked chapel door with a ferocity that was close to hatred.

Then, as if by mutual agreement—though no words were spoken—the pallbearers picked up the casket and carried it to the middle of the campus and put it down gently beneath The Sojourner, whose heavy, flower-lit leaves hovered over it like the inverted peaks of a mother's half-straightened kinky hair. Instead of flowers the students, as if they had planned it, quickly made wreaths from Sojourner's fallen leaves, and The Sojourner herself, ever generous to her children, dropped a leaf on the chest of The Wild Child, who wore for the first time, in her casket, a set of new clothes.

The students sang through tears that slipped like melting pellets of sleet down their grieved and angered cheeks:

"We shall overcome . . .
We shall overcome . . .

We shall overcome, someday . . .
Deep in my heart, I do believe . . .
We shall overcome, someday . . ." ©

That night, after The Wild Child was buried in an overgrown corner of a local black cemetery, students, including Anne-Marion, noted on Saxon campus for the first time in its long, placid, impeccable history, and the only thing they managed to destroy was The Sojourner. Though Meridian begged them to dismantle the president's house instead, in a fury of confusion and frustration they worked all night, and chopped and sawed down, level to the ground, that mighty, ancient, sheltering music tree.

"Have You Stolen Anything?"

Meridian was conscious always of a feeling of guilt, even as a child. Yet she did not know of what she might be guilty. When she tried to express her feelings to her mother, her mother would only ask: "Have you stolen anything?"

Her mother was not a woman who should have had children. She was capable of thought and growth and action only if unfettered by the needs of dependents, or the demands, requirements, of a husband. Her spirit was of such fragility that the slightest impact on it caused a shattering beyond restoration.

In the final days of her young adulthood she had known the luxury of lying in bed as late at nine or ten o'clock on Saturdays, and the joy of earning money as a schoolteacher. She had known the freedom of thinking out the possibilities of her life. They were actually two: She might stay in her home town and teach or she might move elsewhere and teach. She never tired of considering which she should do. This period of her life passed too quickly, so quickly she had not had time to properly value it. There had been a delight in her independence, an adventure in the fingering of her possibilities, but she wanted more of life to happen to her. More richness, more texture. She had begun to look about her for an increase in felicity over what she had. She noticed that other girls were falling in love, getting married. It seemed to produce a state of euphoria in them. She became unsure that her own way of living was as pleasant as she thought it was. It seemed to have an aimlessness to it that did not lead anywhere. Day followed day, and the calm level of her pleasures as a single woman remained constant. Certainly she never reached euphoria. And she wanted euphoria to add to the other good feelings she had.

Of course as a teacher she earned both money and respect. This mattered to her. But there grew in her a feeling that the mothers of her pupils, no matter that they envied her her clothes, her speech, her small black car, pitied her. And in their harried or passive but always overweight and hideously dressed figures she began to suspect a mysterious inner life, secret from her, that made them willing, even happy, to endure.

The man she married, Meridian's father, was also a schoolteacher. He taught history classes in the room next to hers. He was quiet and clean and sincere. They could talk together and were friends long before she felt a toleration for his personal habits that she identified as Love. He was a dreamy, unambitious person even then, who walked over the earth unhurriedly, as if conscious of every step and the print his footsteps would leave in the dirt. He cried as he broke into her body, as she was to cry later when their children broke out of it.

She could never forgive her community, her family, his family, the whole world, for not warning her against children. For a year she had seen some increase in her happiness: She enjoyed joining her body to her husband's in sex, and enjoyed having someone with whom to share the minute occurrences of her day. But in her first pregnancy she became distracted from who she was. As divided in her mind as her body was divided, between what part was herself and what part was not. Her frail independence gave way to the pressures of motherhood and she learned—much to her horror and amazement—that she was not even allowed to be resentful that she was "caught." That her personal life was over. There was no one she could cry out to and say "It's not fair!" And in understanding this, she understood a look she saw in the other women's eyes. The mysterious inner life that she had imagined gave them a secret joy was simply a full knowledge of the fact that they were dead, living just enough for their children. They, too, had found no one to whom to shout "It's not fair!" The women who now had eight, twelve, fifteen children: People made jokes about them, but she could feel now that such jokes were obscene; it was like laughing at a person who is being buried alive, walled away from her own life, brick by brick.

That was the beginning of her abstraction. When

her children were older and not so burdensome—and they were burdens to her always—she wanted to teach again but could not pass the new exams and did not like the new generation of students. In fact, she discovered she had no interest in children, until they were adults; then she would pretend to those she met that she remembered them. She learned to make paper flowers and prayer pillows from tiny scraps of cloth, because she needed to feel something in her hands. She never learned to cook well, she never learned to braid hair prettily or to be in any other way creative in her home. She could have done so, if she had wanted to. Creativity was in her, but it was refused expression. It was all deliberate. A war against those to whom she could not express her anger or shout, "It's not fair!"

With her own daughter she certainly said things she herself did not believe. She refused help and seemed, to Meridian, never to understand. But all along she understood perfectly.

It was for stealing her mother's serenity, for shattering her mother's emerging self, that Meridian felt guilty from the very first, though she was unable to understand how this could possibly be her fault.

When her mother asked, without glancing at her, "Have you stolen anything?" a stillness fell over Meridian and for seconds she could not move. The question literally stopped her in her tracks.

Gold

One day when Meridian was seven she found a large chunk of heavy metal. It was so thickly encrusted with dirt that even when she had washed it the metal did not shine through. Yet she knew metal was there, because it was so heavy. Finally, when she had dried off the water, she took a large file and filed away some of the rust. To her amazement what she had found was a bar of yellow gold. Bullion they called it in the movies. She filed a spot an inch square and ran with it (heavy as it was) to her mother, who was sitting on the back porch shelling peas.

"I've found some gold!" she shouted. "Gold!" And she placed the large heavy gold bar in her mother's lap.

"Move that thing," her mother said sharply. "Don't you see I'm trying to get these peas ready for supper?"

"But it's gold!" she insisted. "Feel how heavy it is. Look how yellow it is. It's gold, and it could make us rich!"

But her mother was not impressed. Neither was

her father or her brothers. She took her bar of gold and filed all the rust off it until it shone like a huge tooth. She put it in a shoe box and buried it under the magnolia tree that grew in the yard. About once a week she dug it up to look at it. Then she dug it up less and less . . . until finally she forgot to dig it up. Her mind turned to other things.

Indians and Ecstasy

Meridian's father had built for himself a small white room like a tool shed in the back yard, with two small windows, like the eyes of an owl, high up under the roof. One summer when the weather was very hot, she noticed the door open and had tiptoed inside. Her father sat at a tiny brown table poring over a map. It was an old map, yellowed and cracked with frayed edges, that showed the ancient settlements of Indians in North America. Meridian stared around the room in wonder. All over the walls were photographs of Indians: Sitting Bull, Crazy Horse, Geronimo, Little Bear, Yellow Flower, and even a drawing of Minnehaha and Hiawatha. There were actual photographs, perhaps priceless ones—which apparently her father had spent years collecting—of Indian women and children looking starved and glassy-eyed and doomed into the camera. There were also books on Indians, on their land rights, reservations, and their wars. As she tiptoed closer to the bookshelves and reached to touch a photograph of a frozen Indian child (whose mother lay beside her in a bloody heap) her father looked up from his map, his face wet with tears, which she mistook, for a moment, for sweat. Shocked and frightened, she ran away.

One day she overheard her parents talking. Her mother was filling fruit jars in the kitchen: "So you've gone and done it, have you?" said her mother, pouring apple slices into the jars with a sloshing noise.

"But the land already belonged to them," her father said, "I was just holding it. The rows of my cabbages and tomatoes run right up along the biggest coil of the Sacred Serpent. That mound is full of dead Indians. Our food is made healthy from the iron and calcium from their bones. Course, since it's a cemetery, we shouldn't own it anyhow."

Before the new road was cut it had not been possible to see the Serpent from the old one. It was news to most of the townspeople that an Indian mound existed there.

"That's disgusting," said her mother. "How can I enjoy my food if you're going to talk about dead Indians?"

"The mound is thousands of years old," said her father. "There's nothing but dust and minerals in there now."

"But to give our land to a naked Indian—"

"Naked? He ain't naked. You believe all that stuff they put on television. He wears a workshirt and blue jeans. His hair is the only thing that looks like Indians look on TV. It's cut off short though, blunt, right behind his jowls, like Johnny Cash's."

"How do you know he ain't a white man playing Indian?"

"Because I know. Grown-up white men don't want to pretend to be anything else. Not even for a minute."

"They'll become anything for as long as it takes to steal some land."

And once Meridian had actually seen the Indian. A tall, heavy man in cowboy boots, his face full of creases like a brown paper bag someone had oiled and pinched a lot of lines in with careless fingers. Squinty black eyes stared with steady intensity into space. He was a wanderer, a mourner, like her father; she could begin to recognize what her father was by looking at him. Only he wandered physically, with his body, not walking across maps with his fingers as her father did. And he mourned dry-eyed. She could not imagine that weathered dusky skin bathed in tears. She could not see his stout dirt-ringed wrists pressing against his silver temples, or flattening in despair the remainder of his still-black hair.

His name was Walter Longknife. Which caused Meridian to swallow her first hello when they were introduced, and he came from Oklahoma. He had started out in an old pickup truck that broke down in the shadow of Stone Mountain. He abandoned it, and was glad, he said—in a slurred voice, as if he were drunk, which he was not—to walk through the land of his ancestors, the Cherokees.

Her father gave Mr. Longknife the deed to the

sixty acres his grandfather acquired after the Civil War. Land too rocky for plowing (until her father and brothers removed all the rocks by hand and wheelbarrow), and too hilly to be easy to sell (prospective buyers always thought the mounds were peculiar hills). Mr. Longknife had kept the paper in his shirt until he was ready to move on—he spent most of the summer camping out on the land—and then he had given it back to her father.

"Other men run away from their families outright," said her mother. "You stay, but give the land under our feet away. I guess that makes you a hero."

"We were part of it, you know," her father said.

"Part of what?"

"Their disappearance."

"Hah," said her mother. "You might have been, but I wasn't even born. Besides, you told me how surprised you were to find that some of them had the nerve to fight for the South in the Civil War. That ought to make up for those few black soldiers who rode against Indians in the Western cavalry."

Her father sighed. "I never said either side was innocent or guilty, just ignorant. They've been a part of it, we've been a part of it, everybody's been a part of it for a long time."

"I know," said her mother, scornfully, "and you would just fly away, if you could."

Meridian's father said that Mr. Longknife had killed a lot of people, mainly Italians, in the Second World War. The reasons he'd done this remained abstract. That was why he was a wanderer. He was looking for reasons, answers, anything to keep his historical vision of himself as a just person from falling apart.

"The answer to everything," said Meridian's mother, "is we live in America and we're not rich."

One day when she was helping her father tie up some running beans, three white men in government-issued trucks—army green with white lettering on the side—came out to the farm. They unloaded a large wire trash basket and two brown picnic tables. They said a bulldozer would be coming the next day. The Indian burial mounds of the Sacred Serpent and her father's garden of prize beans, corn and squash were to be turned into a tourist attraction, a public park.

When her father went to the county courthouse with his deed, the officials said they could offer only token payment; that, and the warning to stay away from Sacred Serpent Park which, now that it belonged to the public, was of course not open to Colored.

Each afternoon after school her father had gone out to the farm. It was beautiful land made more impressive by the five-hundred-yard Sacred Serpent that formed a curving, twisting hill beyond the corn. The garden itself was in rich, flat land that fitted into the curves of the Sacred Serpent like the waves of the ocean fit the shore. Across from the Serpent and the garden was a slow-moving creek that was brown and sluggish and thick, like a stream of liquid snuff. Meridian had always enjoyed being on the farm with him, though they rarely talked. Her brothers were not interested in farming, had no feeling for the land or for Indians or for crops. They ate the fresh produce their father provided while talking of cars and engines and tires and cut-rate hubcaps. They considered working at gas stations a step up. Anything but being farmers. To them the word "farm" was actually used as a curse word.

"Aw, go on back to the *farm,*" they growled over delicious meals.

But Meridian grieved with her father about the loss of the farm, now Sacred Serpent Park. For she understood his gifts came too late and were refused, and his pleasures were stolen away.

Where the springing head of the Sacred Serpent crossed the barbed-wire fence of the adjoining farm, it had been flattened years before by a farmer who raised wheat. This was long before Meridian or her father was born. Her father's grandmother, a woman it was said of some slight and harmless madness, and whose name was Feather Mae, had fought with her husband to save the snake. He had wanted to flatten his part of the burial mound as well and scatter the fragmented bones of the Indians to the winds. "It may not mean anything to you to plant food over other folks' bones," Feather Mae had told her husband, "but if you do you needn't expect me to eat another mouthful in your house!"

It was whispered too that Feather Mae had been very hot, and so Meridian's great-grandfather had not liked to offend her, since he could not bear to suffer the lonely consequences.

She had liked to go there, Feather Mae had, and sit on the Serpent's back, her long legs dangling while she sucked on a weed stem. She was becoming a woman—this was before she married Meridian's insatiable great-grandfather—and would soon be married, soon be expecting, soon be like her own mother, a strong silent woman who seemed always to be washing or ironing or cooking or rousing her family from naps to go back to work in the fields. Meridian's great-grandmother dreamed, with the sun across her legs and her black, moon-bright face open to the view.

One day she watched some squirrels playing up and down the Serpent's sides. When they disappeared she rose and followed them to the center of the Serpent's coiled tail, a pit forty feet deep, with smooth green sides. When she stood in the center of the pit, with the sun blazing down directly over her, something extraordinary happened to her. She felt as if she had stepped into another world, into a different kind of air. The green walls began to spin, and her feeling rose to such a high pitch the next thing she knew she was getting up off the ground. She knew she had fainted but she felt neither weakened nor ill. She felt renewed, as from some strange spiritual intoxication. Her blood made warm explosions through her body, and her eyelids stung and tingled.

Later, Feather Mae renounced all religion that was not based on the experience of physical ecstasy—thereby shocking her Baptist church and its unsympathetic congregation—and near the end of her life she loved walking nude about her yard and worshiped only the sun.

This was the story that was passed down to Meridian.

It was to this spot, the pit, that Meridian went often. Seeking to understand her great-grandmother's ecstasy and her father's compassion for people dead centuries before he was born, she watched him enter the deep well of the Serpent's coiled tail and return to his cornfield with his whole frame radiating brightness like the space around a flame. For Meridian, there was at first a sense of vast isolation. When she raised her eyes to the pit's rim high above her head she saw the sky as completely round as the bottom of a bowl, and the clouds that drifted slowly over her were like a mass of smoke cupped in downward-slanting palms. She was a dot, a speck in creation, alone and hidden. She had contact with no other living thing; instead she was surrounded by the dead. At first this frightened her, being so utterly small, encircled by ancient silent walls filled with bones, alone in a place not meant for her. But she remembered Feather Mae and stood patiently, willing her fear away. And it had happened to her.

From a spot at the back of her left leg there began a stinging sensation, which, had she not been standing so purposely calm and waiting, she might have dismissed as a sign of anxiety or fatigue. Then her right palm, and her left, began to feel as if someone had slapped them. But it was in her head that the lightness started. It was as if the walls of earth that enclosed her rushed outward, leveling themselves at a dizzying rate, and then spinning wildly, lifting her out of her body and giving her the feeling of flying. And in this movement she saw the faces of her family, the branches of trees, the wings of birds, the corners of houses, blades of grass and petals of flowers rush toward a central point high above her and she was drawn with them, as whirling, as bright, as free, as they. Then the outward flow, the rush of images, returned to the center of the pit where she stood, and what had left her at its going was returned. When she came back to her body—and she felt sure she had left it—her eyes were stretched wide open, and they were dry, because she found herself staring directly into the sun.

Her father said the Indians had constructed the coil in the Serpent's tail in order to give the living a sensation similar to that of dying: The body seemed to drop away, and only the spirit lived, set free in the world. But she was not convinced. It seemed to her that it was a way the living sought to expand the consciousness of being alive, there where the ground about them was filled with the dead. It was a possibility they discussed, alone in the fields. Their secret: that they both shared the peculiar madness of her great-grandmother. It sent them brooding at times over the meaning of this. At other times they rejoiced over so tangible a connection to the past.

Later in her travels she would go to Mexico to a

mountain that contained at its point only the remains of an ancient altar, the origin of which no one was certain. She would walk up a steep stair made of stones to the pinnacle of the altar and her face would disappear into the clouds, just as the faces of ancient priests had seemed to disappear into the heavens to the praying followers who knelt in reverence down below. There would again be a rushing out from her all that was surrounding, all that she might have touched, and again she would become a speck in the grand movement of time. When she stepped upon the earth again it would be to feel the bottoms of her feet curl over the grass, as if her feet were those of a leopard or a bear, with curving claws and bare rough pads made sensitive by long use.

In the Capital's museum of Indians she peered through plate glass at the bones of a warrior, shamelessly displayed, dug up in a crouched position and left that way, his front teeth missing, his arrows and clay pipes around him. At such sights she experienced nausea at being alive.

When blacks were finally allowed into Sacred Serpent Park, long after her father's crops had been trampled into dust, she returned one afternoon and tried in vain to relive her earlier ecstasy and exaltation. But there were people shouting and laughing as they slid down the sides of the great Serpent's coil. Others stood glumly by, attempting to study the meaning of what had already and forever been lost.

English Walnuts

"Why are you always so sourfaced about it?" some boy would breathe into her bosom in the back seat of his car during the fifties. "Can't you *smile* some? I mean, is it gon' kill you?"

Her answer was a shrug.

Later on she would frown even more when she realized that her mother, father, aunts, friends, passers-by—not to mention her laughing sister—had told her nothing about what to expect from men, from sex. Her mother never even used the word, and her lack of information on the subject of sex was accompanied by a seeming lack of concern about her daughter's morals. Having told her absolutely nothing, she had expected her to *do* nothing. When Meridian left the house in the evening with her "boyfriend"—her current eager, hot-breathing lover, who always drove straight to the nearest lovers' lane or its equivalent, which in her case was the clump of bushes behind the city dump—her mother only cautioned her to "be sweet." She did not realize this was a euphemism for "Keep your panties up and your dress down," an expression she *had* heard and been puzzled by.

And so, while not enjoying it at all, she had had sex as often as her lover wanted it, sometimes every single night. And, since she *had* been told by someone that one's hips become broader after sex, she looked carefully in her mirror each morning before she caught the bus to school. Her pregnancy came as a total shock.

They lived, she and the latest lover, in a small house not a mile from the school. He married her, as he had always promised he would "if things went wrong." She had listened to this promise for almost two years (while he milked the end of his Trojans for signs of moisture). It had meant nothing because she could not conceive of anything going more wrong than the wrong she was already in. She could not understand why she was doing something with such frequency that she did not enjoy.

His name was Eddie. She did not like the name and didn't know why. It seemed the name of a person who would never amount to much, though "Edward" would have suited her no better.

As her lover, Eddie had had certain lovable characteristics—some of which he retained. He was good-looking and of the high school hero type. He was tall, with broad shoulders, and even though his skin was dark brown (and delicious that way) there was something of the prevailing white cheerleader's delight about him; there was a square regularity about his features, a pugness to his nose. He was, of course, good at sports and excelled in basketball.

And she had loved to watch him make baskets from the center of the gymnasium floor. When he scored he smiled across at her, and the envy of the other girls kept her attentive in her seat.

His hair was straight up, like a brush—neither kinky nor curly. A black version of the then popular crew cut. He wore brown loafers, too, with money in them. And turtlenecks—when they were popular—and the most gorgeous light-blue jeans. Which, she was to learn, required washing and starching and ironing every week, as his mother had done, for dirty jeans were not yet the fashion. His eyes were nice—black and warm; his teeth, perfect. She loved the way his breath remained sweet—like a cow's, she told him, smiling fondly.

Being with him did a number of things for her. Mainly, it saved her from the strain of responding to other boys or even noting the whole category of Men. This was worth a great deal, because she was afraid of men—and was always afraid until she was taken under the wing of whoever wandered across her defenses to become—in a remarkably quick time—her lover. This, then, was probably what sex meant to her; not pleasure, but a sanctuary in which her mind was freed of any consideration for all the other males in the universe who might want anything of her. It was resting from pursuit.

Once in her "sanctuary" she could, as it were, look out at the male world with something approaching equanimity, even charity; even friendship. For she could make male friends only when she was sexually involved with a lover who was always near—if only in the way the new male friends thought of her as "So-an-so's Girl."

Her mother was long-suffering, typically, about the marriage; What had she ever done? and so forth. Then dedicated to the well-being of the beginning small family. Eddie was a good boy, it was argued, it was agreed—in her family's estimation. And he was, by several of the prevailing standards: He was always clean—he bathed, in summer, two or three times a week. His pants, jeans and Sunday, were creased *always.* His shirts starched and not in loud colors. His white buckskin shoes were dirty only when it became the fashion for them to be dirty. When the fashion said otherwise, the buckskins absorbed one bottle of white polish a week. And Eddie was smart: He made B's and an A in Band. He might become a businessman like his father, who worked in his own lumber company. He did not drop out of school when he got married, but simply worked overtime at the restaurant where he had previously worked after school. He had absorbed the belief, prevalent in all their homes, that without at least a high school diploma, a person would never amount to anything. He was even sorry she was expelled from school because of the pregnancy.

"Do you forgive me?" he asked, burrowing his bristly head into her lap.

"Forgive you for what?" It had not occurred to her to blame *him.* She felt, being pregnant, almost as if she'd contracted a communicable disease, that the germs had been in the air and that her catching the disease was no one's fault.

"You know I've always required a lot."

"Always?"

"I did it the first time when I was nine, standing on top of a washtub, under the girl's window."

They laughed. "Did you know what you were doing?"

"A balancing act. But it *felt* so good!"

When she was not nauseous or throwing up, they laughed a lot, though there was a dizziness about it for her, the laughter seemed muted, as if she did it underwater, and the echo of it whirled sluggishly through her head.

They lived simply. She became drawn into the life of his family. Became "another daughter" to his mother. Listened politely to his father's stories of his exploits during the days when black people were sure enough chicken-shit. *Considered* chicken-shit, he added. It was her mother-in-law—a plump, rosy-brown woman with one breast, the other lost to cancer—who told her the "mysteries" of life. Astonishing her with such facts as: It is not possible to become pregnant if love is made standing up. Together they bought cloth to make the baby's clothes. Shopped for secondhand furniture, bought quantities of seasonal foods the two households could share.

And through it all, she sat in the small house not a mile from the school and never thought about the baby at all—unless her mother-in-law called and mentioned it, or something to do with it. She knew she did not want it. But even this was blurred. How could she not want something she was not even sure she was having? Yet she *was* having it, of course. She grew and grew and grew, as pregnant women will. Her skin, always smooth as velvet, became blotchy, her features blunted; her face looked bloated, tight.

She did not, also, think of Eddie very much. She woke to his sweet breath on her face every morning—and wondered who, really, he was. What he was doing there in bed with her. Or she lay with him quietly, after making love, and enjoyed the incredible warmth of his very beautiful young body. So nearly black, so glowing and healthy, so *slim* now, next to hers. She loved the warmth, would do anything for it, his gentleness. She was grateful that he was willing to work so hard for their future, while she could not even recognize it.

"One day," he said over lunch, "we'll have a house like Mr. Yateson's. It will have cactus plants around it and a sky-blue driveway and painted blue trim. In the dining room there'll be a chandelier like the ones in Joan Crawford movies. And there'll be carpeting wall to wall and all the rooms will be different colors."

Mr. Yateson was the principal of their school. His brand-new house, floating on the bright-blue driveway and concrete walks that encircled it, sat back from a dirt road that was impassable when it rained and made Meridian think of a fancy-dressed lady without shoes standing in a puddle of mud.

"Um *hum,*" she would nod vaguely at Eddie's dream.

At the restaurant he worked as a waiter and sometimes short-order cook—hard work, little pay. And yet he was always patient and gentle with her, protective. If he worried he kept it from her, justifying his silence by her "condition." The worries he was unable to hide were about small things that bothered him: the ironing of his clothes, and even her own, which she did not do nearly as well as his mother (who, finally, in the last stages of her daughter-in-law's pregnancy, began to collect their dirty clothes each Wednesday to bring them back on Friday stainless and pale from bleach); the cooking, which she was too queasy to do at all; and the sex, which she did not seem (he said) interested in.

One night as he climbed over her—because he could only make love to her by beginning his assault from her left side—he said:

"And tonight, please, open your legs all the way."

"What do you mean, open my legs?" she asked.

"I have to fight to get your legs open; you know that as well as I do. They're like somebody starched them shut."

She had not been aware that she locked her legs. Now that he had pointed it out to her, however, she found she closed them tighter than ever.

"You just don't care about it any more," he moaned, burying his head in the pillow next to hers.

In fact, this last worry surprised her. She did not

see how he could feel she was less interested in sex, for she felt she had never shown anything approaching interest. Nor could she imagine why any woman *should.* She loved the warmth, the lying together, the peace. She endured the sex because it gave her these things. She would have been just as happy, happier, without it. But he did not understand this and would sometimes seem hurt and complain. She did not know what to do, so of course she put the blame on any handy thing: her big stomach, the queasiness, the coming baby, old wives' tales that forbade intercourse until three months after the baby was born (a fact she learned from his mother: that intercourse any earlier weakened one's brain).

By that time—and it did not surprise her—he had a woman who loved sex, and was able to get as much of it as he wanted every night.

But he was "good" to her, even then. He did not "cheat" and "beat" her both, which meant he was "good" to her, according to her mother, his mother, the other women in the neighborhood and in fact just about everyone she knew, who seemed always to expect the two occurrences together, like the twin faces of a single plague.

But had she lost interest in sex completely? She didn't know. It was simply that sex was now something that she knew and thought she understood. Before it had been curiosity about her body's power. Nor was her response to Eddie's lovemaking as uncomplicated as he appeared to think.

She had not been wandering exactly on those afternoons she had found herself in front of Daxter's funeral home—that huge, snowy, two-storied building that stood on a hill between a church and an all-night café. Daxter's was owned by George Daxter, an obese half-white man in his fifties. His mother, so the story went, was white. When her parents found she was pregnant by the black man who worked for them, they shut her up in the cellar and threw away the key. They fed her pig bran and a little watery milk. When Daxter was born he was thrown out into the street with the rest of the trash. He was raised by an old woman who later died of ptomaine poisoning. She had eaten some sour, rotten tomatoes Daxter gave her.

Daxter had been after Meridian since she was twelve years old. She would visit the funeral home on Saturday afternoons, as everybody did to see who was new in the viewing room. Daxter would entice her into the small back office where he kept a long sofa and two soft chairs. At first she thought Daxter generous: He gave her candy for a swift, exploratory feel. When she became older—fifteen or so—he would take out his wallet crammed with money, and leave it on the sofa between them while he felt her breasts and tried to pull her onto his lap. The only part she liked was when he sucked her nipples, and she liked to hear his breathing, like his throat was closing, when she let one chubby hand touch the bottom of her panties. She could sit, holding his head against her breasts—where he busily and noisily sucked—and feel the hot throbbing of his passion almost enter her. But his obesity, in the end, was distasteful to her. She had heard that fat men had short, stunted penises. She imagined Daxter's penis to look like an English walnut.

When Daxter was not around she allowed herself to be chased around the embalming table by his young assistant, an almost handsome man, but dissipated and with a face that—as the saying went—*begged* for pussy. He thought of nothing else. His tool of seduction (his description) was his voice, which he used to describe the act of intercourse. Holding her with her back tight against him so that his penis was like a hard, live bedpost against her hips, he would whisper in her ear: "Think of how it would feel," he would urge, grabbing one, then both, of her nipples, "to have this big, black, long, ummm . . ." and he would press the bedpost against her—"inside you. Slippin' in and slippin' out."

She hated him but was fascinated; she was also far from immune to the voice. The Assistant would manipulate her breasts and cram her between his legs and rub her so against him that her panties became flooded with the residue of her resistance. The Assistant was very clever and so never actually forced her beyond a certain point, but each time he left her with one of his little homilies: "Experience is the best, the *only,* teacher," and "Just looking at water will never teach you to swim."

One day The Assistant, who knew (he said) how

much she wanted to, was *ready* to, be fucked—if not by him then by the Voice, the Bedpost—arranged for her to watch him while he seduced another schoolgirl (the same girl, in fact, who did baby-sitting for his wife). He did it in the small shed where the wicker baskets were stored. She watched because she was curious, wanted to learn without doing, if possible, and because she had nothing better to do on a hot Wednesday afternoon.

The Assistant began by standing with his bedpost against the back of the girl. She was about sixteen, and wore loafers and a red cardigan sweater turned backward with a neat little white collar. Her small brown hands kept checking the collar to be sure it had not become unfastened by the stripping quality of The Assistant's words. His hands were elsewhere. Already under the cardigan, kneading the nipples—then into her pants as her skirt fell to the floor. Then he hoisted her up onto the table and began to fuck her standing up. Then up on the table. The girl was bucking up and down as fast as she could, as if she feared to break a rhythm she had learned by heart. The Voice fucked more slowly, expertly, like a machine, and the Voice never stopped talking. At the end he watched her as if from a distance, his voice a monotone, his face greedy, obscene and ugly. When the girl tried to bury her face in his chest and force his arms around her, he pushed her away.

The Assistant said later that the girl was his now whenever he wanted her, because he had discovered a secret few men knew: how to make a woman come by using nothing but his penis and his beautiful voice. These were his gifts, The Assistant said, more skillful than the suppleness of wrist required to extract cold blood from a cadaver's vein. And what had she thought of his performance? She was willing to continue their meetings on one condition, she told him. What is that? he eagerly asked, sucking a lemon for his throat. If you hold me in your arms, she said casually, you must promise not to talk.

Of course she had given up Daxter and The Assistant when she became involved with Eddie—well, not just at first. She was guilty of having tried to use them to discover him, what he wanted from her; and yet their pawing over her and her refusal to do anything more than tease them had seemingly separated her from her young husband forever. For as much as she wanted to, she—her body, that is—never had any intention of *giving in.* She was suspicious of pleasure. She might approach it, might gaze on it with longing, but retreat was inevitable. Besides, Eddie did not seriously expect more than "interest" from her. She perceived there might be something more; but for him, it was enough that his pleasure should please her. Understanding this, they never discussed anything beyond her attitude.

The Happy Mother

She had been in hard labor for a day and a half. Then, when she brought the baby home, it had suffered through a month of colic, gasping and screaming and robbing her of sleep. She was so exhausted it was futile to attempt to think straight, or even to think at all. It took everything she had to tend to the child, and she had to do it, her body prompted not by her own desires, but by her son's cries. So this, she mumbled, lurching toward his crib in the middle of the night, is what slavery is like. Rebelling, she began to dream each night, just before her baby sent out his cries, of ways to murder him.

She sat in the rocker Eddie had bought and stroked her son's back, her fingers eager to scratch him out of her life. She realized he was even more helpless than herself, and yet she would diaper him roughly, yanking his fat brown legs in the air, because he looked like his father and because everyone who came to visit assumed she loved him, and because he did not feel like anything to her but a ball and chain.

The thought of murdering her own child eventually frightened her. To suppress it she conceived, quite consciously, methods of killing herself. She found it pleasantly distracting to imagine herself stiff and oblivious, her head stuck in an oven. Or coolly out of it, a hole through the roof of her mouth. It seemed to her that the peace of the dead was truly blessed, and each day she planned a new way of approaching it. Because of her growing reliance on suicide, the thought of it, she was able to function very well. She was told by everyone that she was an exemplary young mother, so mature, so calm. This pleased her because it was so amusing. She delighted in the praise. As her face grew warmer and warmer she began to giggle—to be praised some more for her good humor.

She felt as though something perched inside her brain was about to fly away. Eddie went to the restaurant, worked, came home (or did not come home), ate, slept, went off to school in the morning, as before. He loved his son, and was good to the child. He bought him the usual stupid presents, showed him off to his parents, took pictures every six weeks and even learned to change the baby's diaper—though he denied this expertise when his friends came to visit.

She wondered sometimes why she still did not love Eddie. It perplexed her. He was still good-looking, still sought after by women (several, by now, had caught him, at least for a time), and he treated her with gentleness and respect. But the longer they lived together the more she became obsessed with the horrible thought that Eddie, like his name, would never be grown up. She thought he would always be a boy. Not that she knew what a man should be; she did not know. She only knew that none of the boys she had dated or been friends with seemed capable of becoming men. She projected first one, then the other, of them into the future. They became older, but still boys. She could imagine them only in positions similar to—if on the surface vastly different from—the one Eddie held at the restaurant. Fetching and carrying and courteously awaiting orders from someone above. She could not imagine one of them becoming, for example, president of the local bank.

This affected her with a kind of lethargy. She could not become active again. She could not move about her own house purposefully. What was the use?

She could, however, criticize. And she began to find fault—with everything. Small things, at first. For starters: Why did his pants and shirts have to be starched and ironed after every second wearing? (By this time his mother had stopped doing the laundry for them.) It did not seem a reasonable answer to her that his mother "had *always* done this," or that he was "*used* to clean clothes." So what? she answered, so was she. But she had learned to wear her clothes longer than two days without changing them. Except for her underwear. And why, she wondered, must he shower for such a long time and fog up the bathroom so that if she came in, even to use the toilet, her hair was ruined by the steam?

And did he still play basketball at school? And was there a point to staying fit? What damn good did he expect it to do?

More seriously: She hated the fact that although he was still in school and she was not, he did not seem to know anything about books—or about the world. She learned more than he knew from watching TV quiz programs.

He was not interested in "education," he said, but in finishing school. She despised this answer because she knew the truth of it. She knew also that it was the aim of everyone in the school, from the principal to the first-graders. In fact, "finishing school" was synonymous with "education." The point was, she did not believe it, now that she was no longer in school. School had been dreary, but only there had she occasionally experienced the quicksilver flash of learning that never came to her now.

She read *Sepia, Tan, True Confessions, Real Romances* and *Jet.* According to these magazines, Woman was a mindless body, a sex creature, something to hang false hair and nails on. Still, they helped her know for sure her marriage was breaking up. She lived with the awareness in her usual fog of unconcern. Yet the break, when it came, was not—as she had feared and sometimes hoped—cataclysmic. In fact, in a way she hardly noticed it. It did not come at once, with a heated argument, fighting, packing or slamming doors. It came in pieces, some larger or smaller than others. It came—on Eddie's part—with a night away here, three or four days absent there, and with a cooling off, slightly, of his usual affectionate attention to the baby. This was the only sign of calculation she could detect on his part. He assumed, naturally, that the baby would remain with her (this was, after all, how such arrangements had *always* gone), and he did not intend to see much more of either of them. On her side there was just—a continuation of her lethargy, an unwillingness to put forth effort for anything.

On the day he left, she had walked past a house, not far from theirs, where—since it was nearly summer—all the doors and windows were open. People, young people, were everywhere. They milled about inside, shouted out of windows to those outside, looked carefree (as childless young people, her own age, always now looked to her) and yet as if sensitive to some outside surveillance beyond her own staring. But she was the only person walking on that street. And she stopped to look only because it was a black family's house, in a black neighborhood, and there were several young white people. And all of the young people were strangely dressed and looked, really, funny and old-timey in the overalls and clodhoppers they wore. Even the girls (and she noticed especially a white girl with long brown hair) were dressed in overalls *with bibs!*

It was something to think about, the day Eddie moved out for good. She could not, somehow, concentrate on the fact of his leaving. She did not know deeply enough what it might mean. *Was* he gone for good? Did he actually take all his clothes—even the starched but unironed shirts balled up in the refrigerator? And who was to play with the baby when he woke up? Eddie usually did, if he had a few minutes between work and school.

Now she sat listlessly, staring at the TV. The house she had passed was on. There was to be a voter registration drive (she wondered what that was) that would begin in the city, at that house, and work its way out to the people in the country. Local blacks, volunteers, were needed. A group of young men made this announcement to a (white) newscaster who looked astonished and held his handkerchief over the mike when he presented it; when he talked into it himself, he removed the handkerchief. Black people were never shown in the news—unless of course they had shot their mothers or raped their bosses' grandparent—and a black person or persons giving a news conference was unheard of. But this concerned her, gathered her attention, only superficially, for all its surprise. It kept her mind somewhere else while she made her hands play with the baby, whom, even then, she had urges to kill. To strangle that soft, smooth, helpless neck, to push down that kinky head into a tub of water, to lock it in its room to starve. It looked at her with apprehension, looked about mournfully for its daddy. She forced herself to think only of the black faces on TV and about the house not far from her own.

The next morning as she lay in bed watching the early news, she was again shown pictures of the house—except now the house no longer existed anywhere but on film. During the night—between three and four A.M.—the house was demolished by firebombs. The bombs, exploding, set fire to—not just that house—the whole cluster of houses on that street. Three small children were injured—no, a flash at the bottom of the screen announced them dead; several grownups were injured. One adult, missing, was assumed dead. The others had somehow escaped. It seems they had posted a guard who was alerted by the sound of a pickup truck stopping several yards from the house and then, in a few minutes, racing off.

This struck her, that they had had a guard. Why did they need a guard? Then, a question more to the point: How had they *known* they would need a guard? Did they know something she did not know? She had lived in this town all her life, but could not have foreseen that the house would be bombed. Perhaps because nothing like this had ever happened before. Not in this town. Or *had* it? She recalled that the night before she had dreamed of Indians. She had thought she had forgotten about them.

And so it was that one day in the middle of April in 1960 Meridian Hill became aware of the past and present of the larger world.

Clouds

Each morning, after the bombing, she took the child—his name was Eddie Jr.—to spend the day with his uncle, his father's baby brother, who was only three years old. Eddie's mother, now forty-nine, had undoubtedly misinterpreted one of her sexual facts: Meridian could never quite believe her when she said she'd planned such a late baby. With Eddie Jr. gone, she returned to the house—now subsidized by her in-laws—and put her feet up against the windowsill in the back bedroom. The window looked out into a small enclosed back yard—usually green, except for the brief winter from December to March—and she attempted to meditate on her condition, unconscious, at first, of what she did. At first it was like falling back into a time that never was, a time of complete rest, like a faint. Her senses were stopped, while her body rested; only in her head did she feel something, and it was a sensation of lightness—a lightness like the inside of a drum. The air inside her head was pure of thought, at first. For hours she sat by the window looking out, but not seeing the pecan trees bending in the wind, or the blue clouded sky, or the grass.

At three o'clock she moved to a side window and watched the children walk by on their way home from school. She watched the young girls, their bodies just forming into women's bodies. Watched how they bent against the wind or held their books in front of them in a gesture of defense, almost of shame. Certainly of fear. Then, in the slightly older ones, there was the beginning pride in their bodies, so that they did not bend against the wind—wind real or wind imaginary—but stood with their breasts as obvious as possible so that the boys, galloping alongside and past them in herds, neighing, in their incoherent, aimless laughter and banter, like young ponies—looked boldly at them and grinned and teased and brought embarrassment and pleasure to the young girls. But, Meridian thought, for all their bodies' assertion, the girls moved protected in a dream. A dream that had little to do with the real boys galloping past them. For they did not perceive them clearly but as they might become in a different world from the one they lived in. Which might explain why she could herself recall nothing of those years, beyond the Saturday afternoons and evenings in the picture show. For it was the picture show that more than anything else filled those bantering, galloping years.

Movies: Rory Calhoun, Ava Gardner, Bette Davis, Slim Pickens. Blondes against brunettes and cowboys against Indians, good men against bad, darker men. This fantasy world made the other world of school—with its monotony and tedium—bearable. The young girls she watched were, for the most part, well brought up. They were polite, they were sweet, they were intelligent. They simply did not know they were living their own lives—between twelve and fifteen—but assumed they lived someone else's. They tried to live the lives of their movie idols; and those lives were fantasy. Not even the white people they watched and tried to become—the actors—lived them.

So they moved, did the young girls outside her window, in the dream of happy endings: of women who had everything, of men who ran the world. So had she.

But these thoughts, which were as random and fleeting as clouds, were simply the outside layer of skin on a very large onion.

She was still only seventeen. A drop-out from high school, a deserted wife, a mother, a daughter-in-law. This being so, in the late afternoons she went to her mother-in-law's house and picked up the child, who did not want to come home.

The Attainment of Good

Her mother's life was sacrifice. A blind, enduring, stumbling—though with dignity (as much as was possible under the circumstances)—through life. She did not appear to understand much beyond what happened in her own family, in the neighborhood and in her church. She did not take extreme positions on anything, unless unreasonably provoked over a long period. Then she spluttered out her rage in barely coherent complaints against—but what *had* her mother complained against? She did not complain against the church because she believed the church building—the mortar and bricks—to be holy; she believed that this holiness had rubbed off from years of scripture reading and impassioned prayers, so that now holiness covered the walls like paint. She thought the church was literally God's house, and believed she felt his presence there when she entered the door; when she stepped back outside there was a different feeling, she believed.

There were many things wrong with the church, of course. One was that the preacher was not usually understandable. That is, his words were not, his sentences were not. For years—thirty of them—she sat every Sunday convinced that this man—whoever was preaching at the time—was instilling in her the words and wisdom of God, when, in fact, every other sentence was incomprehensible. Preachers preached in a singsong voice that was rhythmic, often majestic and always passionate. They made elaborate modern examples from ancient texts. They were musicians. They were poets. She was aroused, her spirit enlarged by a desire to be good. (For that, she knew, was what all the words of God led to, whether she could hear them clearly or not.) To the attainment of Good. To a state of righteousness. She did not learn very much beyond a rudimentary knowledge of the birth and crucifixion of Christ (which seemed to have occurred so close together in History she often wondered if Christ had had a childhood), and of the miracle of Ezekiel's wheel (whose meaning was that even before the airplane man could get off the ground if he just had Faith), and of the Exodus, under the command of Moses, of the children of Israel (a race, unfortunately, no longer extant). The songs she understood. They allowed every sinner to sing of her sins to high heaven without the risk of being taken to task personally.

Mrs. Hill did not complain about anything political because she had no desire to understand politics. She had never voted in her life. Meridian grew up thinking voting days—with their strewn banners and long lines of people—were for celebration of some kind of weird festival especially for white people, who, grim and tight, disappeared into dreary, curtained boxes and emerged seconds later looking strongly relieved. Nor did Mrs. Hill complain about the education of her children. She believed the teachers to be eminently qualified (that is, more qualified than she herself) to teach them. If she felt contempt for them because she could no longer count herself among them and because they were poor housekeepers, she kept it very carefully to herself. She respected schoolteachers as a class but despised them as individuals. At the same time, she needed to believe in their infallibility. Otherwise she could not attempt to copy the clothes they wore, the way they fixed their hair or the way they spoke—or the authority with which they were able to confront and often dominate less well educated men.

In fact, she complained only about her husband, whose faults, she felt, more than made up for her ignorance of whatever faults might exist elsewhere.

In the ironing of her children's clothes she expended all the energy she might have put into openly loving them. Her children were spotless wherever they went. In their stiff, almost inflexible garments, they were enclosed in the starch of her anger, and had to keep their distance to avoid providing the soggy wrinkles of contact that would cause her distress.

Awakening

A month after the bombing Meridian walked through the gate of a house and knocked on the door.

"I've come to volunteer," she said to the dark young man staring at her there.

What was she volunteering into? She had no real idea. Something about the bombing had attracted her, the obliteration of the house, the knowledge that had foreseen this destruction. What would these minds, these people, be like?

"Swinburn," said the boy who opened the door, "look what the good Lord done gone and sent us." He was short and stout with puffy brown eyes behind his glasses. His smile was warm and welcoming, and when he preceded Meridian into the room she noticed he dipped and bobbed ever so slightly like a man pulling a dog on a leash.

Swinburn rose from a table in the back of the room near the window. "Thank God," he said. "Allah be praised and paid. Come on in here, lady, and let me ask you something. Can you type?"

"No," said Meridian, who had taken typing for

three months before she'd started having morning sickness—all-day sickness, in her case.

"Can you learn quickly?" A young man, older than the other two, stood in the doorway. He was looking at her in a steady, cool, appraising way, and held some papers in his hands. She could not help staring at his nose, which was high-bridged and keen, and seemed to have come straight off the faces of Ethiopian warriors, whose photographs she had seen. It was wonderfully noble, she thought, and gave the young man an arrogant look. He was dressed in blue jeans and a polo shirt and his shirt front was covered with buttons. That he wore lots of buttons struck Meridian as odd, too playful, for such a cool, serious man. She wanted buttons like that, though. When he came closer she especially liked the large one that showed a black hand and a white hand shaking, although since the colors were flat the hands did not seem, on closer inspection, to be shaking at all; they seemed to be merely touching palms, or in the act of sliding away from each other.

"Yes," she said, "I guess I could learn."

The one called Swinburn was busy pecking out something on the typewriter in front of him, his thin back bent over, his ribs showing beneath his faded shirt. He was very dark brown, with full, neatly curved lips and large eyes behind wireless glasses that further magnified them. When he spoke, his deep voice coming up from the thin cavern of his chest was extraordinary. The timbre was so deep it seemed to make things rattle in the room.

When he made an error typing he pulled at his short, rough hair. He was speeding up his pecking, now that he knew she was looking at him, but the number of errors he made soon caused him to jump up and offer his chair to her.

"Don't you want to know my name?"

"Oh," rumbled Swinburn, "I'm sorry. It's just that we've been so busy since the bombing. Getting another house, trying to raise money . . . My name is, uh, Swinburn, that's Chester Gray" (indicating one of the other young men).

"*Et je m'appelle* Truman Held," said the young man with the nose.

The other two men laughed at him: "It even rhymes!" they said. But Meridian was puzzled. Perhaps they were laughing at her, too, because she had not understood what had been said. She told them her name, they grunted and then turned away, except for Swinburn.

"This is just a petition," he said, standing over her. "You know about the bombing? We're trying to find out how many local people would be interested in marching downtown to protest. Just type out what I've written there, and I'll take it over to the school and see if I can have it mimeographed."

"You mean at *our* school?" she asked.

"Of course," said Swinburn.

"They won't do it over there."

"Why not," asked Swinburn.

"I can't say why not," said Meridian, "all I know is they won't do it. They won't even let us wear shorts on the Easter egg hunt."

"Well, type it anyway," said Swinburn. "Some way or other we'll get enough copies made."

"Meridian typed and typed, until her back seemed to be cracking and her eyes smarted. Her typing was horrible, and she felt ashamed of the amount of paper she was using. After an hour she was able to lay out a perfect copy of the petition, except that she'd put an "e" on Negro.

"It's all right," said Swinburn, crossing out the "e" with a thick, blunt pen, so that the beauty of the finished product was hopelessly marred, "all you need is practice."

Battle Fatigue

Truman Held was the first of the Civil Rights workers—for that's what they were called—who began to mean something to her, though it was months after their initial meeting that she knew. It was not until one night when first he, then she, was arrested for demonstrating outside the local jail, and then beaten.

There had been a Freedom march to the church, a prayer by the Reverend in charge, Freedom songs, several old women testifying (mainly about conditions inside the black section of the jail, which caused Meridian's body to twitch with dread) and finally, a plan of what their strategy was to be, and the singing of "Ain't Gonna Let Nobody Turn Me Round."

The strategy was for a midnight march, with candles, across the street from the jail by the people who had not been arrested earlier, of whom Truman was one. The strategy was, in fact, for everyone not formerly arrested to be so. This was in protest against the town's segregated hospital facilities. It was also an attempt to have the earlier demonstrators released from jail. But even as she marched, singing, to the courthouse square, which was across from the jail, Meridian could not figure out how it was supposed to work. The earlier demonstrators, she felt sure, would not be set free because a few singing people stood peacefully across from the jail. And the jail was too small to accommodate any more bodies. It must already be jammed.

They had been singing for only a few minutes when the town became alive with flashing lights. Police cars came from everywhere. Dozens of state troopers surrounded them, forming a wall between them and the jail. She noticed they really *did* have crew cuts, they really *did* chew gum. Next, the jailhouse door was opened and the earlier demonstrators came wearily out, their faces misshapen from swellings and discolored from bruises. Truman limped along with the rest, moving in great pain and steadily muttering curses as the line of troopers hurried them relentlessly out of the square. It was a few seconds before Meridian understood that it was now their turn.

As soon as this line was out of sight, the troopers turned on them, beating and swinging with their bludgeons. One blow knocked Meridian to the ground, where she was trampled by people running back and forth over her. But there was nowhere to run. Only the jail door was open and unobstructed. Within minutes they had been beaten inside, where the sheriff and his deputies waited to finish them. And she realized why Truman was limping. When the sheriff grabbed her by the hair and someone else began punching her and kicking her in the back, she did not even scream, except very intensely in her own mind, and the scream was Truman's name. And what she meant by it was not even that she was in love with him: What she meant by it was that they were at a time and a place in History that forced the trivial to fall away—and they were absolutely together.

Later that summer, after another demonstration, she saw him going down a street that did not lead back to the black part of town. His eyes were swollen and red, his body trembling, and he did not recognize her or even see her. She knew his blankness was battle fatigue. They all had it. She was as weary as anyone, so that she spent a good part of her time in tears. At first she had burst into tears whenever something went wrong or someone spoke unkindly or even sometimes if they spoke, period. But now she was always in a state of constant tears, so that she could do whatever she was doing—canvassing, talking at rallies, tying her sneakers, laughing—while tears rolled slowly and ceaselessly down her cheeks. This might go on for days, or even weeks. Then, suddenly, it would stop, and some other symptom would appear. The shaking of her hands, or the twitch in her left eye. Or the way she would sometimes be sure she'd heard a shot and feel the impact of the bullet against her back; then she stood absolutely still, waiting to feel herself fall.

She went up to a yard with an outdoor spigot and soaked the bottom of her blouse in water. When she came back down to the street to wipe the tear gas from Truman's eyes, he was gone. A police car was careening down the street. She stood in the street feeling the cool wet spot on her side, wondering what to do.

The majority of black townspeople were sympathetic to the Movement from the first, and told Meridian she was doing a good thing: typing, teaching illiterates to read and write, demonstrating against segregated facilities and keeping the Movement house open when the other workers returned to school. Her mother, however, was not sympathetic.

"As far as I'm concerned," said Mrs. Hill, "you've wasted a year of your life, fooling around with those people. The papers say they're crazy. God separated the sheeps from the goats and the black folks from the white. And me from anybody that acts as foolish as they do. It never bothered *me* to sit in the back of the bus, you get just as good a view and you don't have all those nasty white asses passing you."

Meridian attempted to ignore her, but her mother would continue. "If somebody thinks he'll have to pee when he gets to town, let him use his own toilet before he leaves home! That's what we did when I was coming up!" Eventually Mrs. Hill would talk herself out.

It had taken Meridian a long time to tell her mother she *was* in the Movement, and by the time she did, her mother already knew. Now she had news that was even more likely to infuriate her. To deliver it, she brought Delores Jones (another Movement worker) and Nelda Henderson, an old playmate, with her. It was cowardly of her, but Meridian could not face her mother alone.

While Meridian was still a student in high school she was tested and informed that, for her area and background, her IQ of 140 was unusually high. She was pregnant at the time, sick as a dog and about to be expelled from school; she had shrugged her shoulders at the news. But now, though she had not completed high school, she was to have—if she wanted it—a chance to go to college. Mr. Yateson told her this, explaining that a unique honor was being bestowed upon her—who might or might not be worthy; after all, nice girls did not become pregnant in high school—and that he expected her to set a high moral standard because she would be representing the kind of bright "product" his "plant" could produce.

He spoke so proprietarily she thought at first he intended to send her to college with his own money. But no. He explained that a generous (and wealthy) white family in Connecticut—who wished to help some of the poor, courageous blacks they saw marching and getting their heads whipped nightly on TV—had decided, as a gesture of their liberality and concern, to send a smart black girl to Saxon College in Atlanta, a school this family had endowed for three generations.

"You don't mean I'm the smartest one you've got!" said Meridian, humbly. But then the thought that this might be true simply because Mr.

Yateson's "plant" generally produced nothing among its "products" but boredom tickled her and she smiled.

Mr. Yateson was annoyed. "In my day," he said, "we didn't reward bad behavior—nor did we think it was funny!"

So then Meridian felt she had to apologize for her smile, even though it had been such a pathetic one, and some of the joy of the experience went out of it for her.

It was Truman who put it back by telling her Saxon College was only two hours away, and just across the street from his own school, R. Baron College, which he attended when he was not working in the Movement out of town. Because of course there was an Atlanta Movement, in which he had already been involved. He and Meridian would see each other every day.

"Mais oui," Truman kept saying, as she looked shyly but happily up at him, "you will be just the Saxon type!"

But then, she had never told him she had a child.

"You have a right to go to college," said Delores. "You're lucky to have the chance." She was slender and brown, with a strong, big nose and eyebrows like black wings. She wore jeans and flowered shirts and was unafraid of everything. "Listen," she said, "it's not every day that somebody's going to care about your high IQ and offer you a scholarship. You ain't no dummy, girl, and don't you even consider acting like one now." They walked up to the front door, Nelda Henderson reaching out to squeeze Meridian's hand.

"No matter what your mother says," Delores continued, "just remember she spends all her time making prayer pillows."

Nelda said nothing about Meridian going to college because she wanted to save her words for Meridian's mother. Nelda cried easily and looked at Delores and Meridian with sad envy. She was pregnant again and it was just beginning to show. When Mrs. Hill came to the door there was a coolness in her response to Nelda's greeting, which brought the always close tears to the surface.

The Hills' house was white on the outside with turquoise shutters. It was cluttered with heavy brown furniture, white porcelain dolls, and churns filled with paper flowers. Dozens of snapshots of other people's children grinned down at them from the walls.

"Well, it can't be moral, that I know. It can't be right to give away your own child." They sat around the dining room table drinking tea. "If the good Lord gives you a child he means for *you* to take care of it."

"The good Lord didn't give it to her," muttered Delores. Delores was intrepid. Meridian loved her.

"But this is the only chance I have, Mama," she said.

"You should have thought about that before."

"I didn't *know* before," she said, looking into her glass. "How can I take care of Eddie Jr. anyway?" she asked. "I can't even take care of myself."

Mrs. Hill frowned. "Do you know how many women have thought that and had to have God make a way? You surprised me," she continued, sighing. "I always thought you were a *good* girl. And all the time, you were fast."

"I was something," said Meridian. "But I didn't even know what fast was. You always talked in riddles. 'Be sweet' 'Don't be fast.' You never made a bit of sense."

"That's right," said Mrs. Hill. "Blame me for trusting you. But I know one thing: Everybody else that slips up like you did *bears* it. You're the only one that thinks you can just outright refuse . . ." Mrs. Hill stopped and wiped her eyes.

"Look at Nelda," she began, "I know *she'd* never . . ."

But Nelda interrupted. "Don't say that, Mrs. Hill," she said, her eyes tearing. "I'd do anything to have a chance to go to college like Meridian. I wish to God I could have made it to junior high."

For a moment, as she looked at Meridian's mother, there was hatred in her sad eyes. Hatred and comprehension of betrayal. She had lived across the street from the Hills all her life. She and Meridian played together in the Hills' back yard, they went to school together. Nelda knew that the information she had needed to get through her adolescence was information Mrs. Hill could have given her.

There had been about Nelda in those days a naive and admirable sweetness, but there was also apparent, if one knew how to recognize such things (and Mrs. Hill might certainly have done so), a premonition of her fall, which grew out of her meek acceptance of her family's burdens. She had been left in charge of her five younger brothers and sisters every day while her mother worked. On Saturdays she struggled to town to do the shopping, the twins racing ahead of her down the street, the two toddlers holding to her arms and the baby strapped to her back. This was Nelda—as pretty, the boys used to say, as an Indian—at fourteen, just before she became pregnant herself.

On Sundays Nelda was free to do as she liked. Her mother did not work then, but spent most of the day—with all her other children neatly dressed and combed—in church. (She was a large, "baldheaded" woman, with massive breasts and a fine contralto singing voice. Her husband had been lost in France during the Second World War, and though only two of her children were his—Nelda and the next oldest child, a boy—they all carried his name. She had lost her hair, bit by bit, during each pregnancy.) Nelda was allowed to spend the day at home washing her hair, making dinner and doing her homework (she made it to school perhaps six times a month, and no truant officer ever knocked on her door), and in the late afternoons she went, with Meridian and Delores, to a movie in town, where the three of them sat in the gallery above the heads of the white movie goers and necked with their boyfriends of the moment.

Meridian knew the father of Nelda's first baby. He was an older boy, in high school, a gentle boy who treated Nelda as if he loved her more than life, which he might have. He bought her combs and blouses and Bermuda shorts, and her first pair of stockings—all from the three-dollar allowance his mother gave him each week plus his earnings from cutting lawns during the summer. While her mother was at work he often came by to cut their grass and stayed to help Nelda give the children supper, baths and put them to bed. Nelda was well into her third month before she realized something was wrong. It started, she confided to Meridian, by her noticing her pee smelled different.

"What do you mean, your *pee* smells different?" Meridian laughed.

"I don't know," Nelda giggled, "but this ain't its usual smell."

They sat on the toilets at school and laughed and laughed.

"You should *want* Eddie Jr.," said Mrs. Hill. "Unless you're some kind of monster. And no daughter of mine is a monster, surely."

Meridian closed her eyes as tight as she could.

Delores cleared her throat. "The only way Meridian can take care of Eddie Jr. is if she moves in here with you and gets a job in somebody's kitchen while you take care of the kid."

"Of course I'll help out," said Mrs. Hill. "I wouldn't let either one of 'em starve, but—" she continued, speaking to Delores as if Meridian were not present, "this is a clean, upright, *Christian* home. We believe in God in this house."

"What's that got to do with anything?" asked Delores, whose face expressed belligerence and confusion. "The last time God had a baby he skipped, too."

Mrs. Hill pretended she wasn't angry and insulted. She smiled at this girl she wanted to hit. "You're not from around here," she said, "everybody knows people from up Atlanta have strange ideas. A lot of you young people have lost your respect for the church. Do you even believe in God?"

"I give it some thought," said Delores.

Mrs. Hill drew in her stomach and crossed her plump arms over it. "I just don't see how you could let another woman raise your child," she said. "It's just selfishness. You ought to hang your head in shame. I have six children," she continued self-righteously, "though I never wanted to have any, and I have raised every one myself."

"You probably could have done the same thing in slavery," said Delores.

"Let's all be monsters!" Delores joked as she and her friends left Mrs. Hill's house, but Meridian and Nelda did not laugh.

She might not have given him away to the people who wanted him. She might have murdered him instead. Then killed herself. They would all have understood this in time. She might have done it that way except for one thing: One day she really looked at her child and loved him with as much love as she loved the moon or a tree, which was a considerable amount of impersonal love. She wanted to know more about his perfect, if unplanned-for, existence.

"Who are you?" she asked him.

"Where were you when I was twelve?"

"Who *are* you?" she persisted, studying his face for signs of fire, watermarks, some scar that would intimate a previous life.

"Were there other people where you were? Did you come from a planet of babies?" She thought she could just imagine him there, on such a planet, pulling the blue grass up by the handfuls.

Now that she looked at him, the child was beautiful. She had thought him ugly, like a hump she must carry on her back.

"You will no longer be called Eddie Jr." she said. "I'll ask them to call you Rundi, after no person, I hope, who has ever lived."

When she gave him away she did so with a light heart. She did not look back, believing she had saved a small person's life.

But she had not anticipated the nightmares that began to trouble her sleep. Nightmares of the child, Rundi, calling to her, crying, suffering unbearable deprivations because she was not there, yet she knew it was just the opposite: Because she was not there he needn't worry, ever, about being deprived. Of his life, for instance. She felt deeply that what she'd done was the only thing, and was right, but that did not seem to matter. On some deeper level than she had anticipated or had even been aware of, she felt condemned, consigned to penitence, for life. The past pulled the present out of shape as she realized that what Delores Jones had said was *not*, in fact, true. If her mother had had children in slavery she would not, automatically, have been allowed to keep them, because they would not have belonged to her but to the white person who "owned" them all. Meridian knew that enslaved women had been made miserable by the sale of their children, that they had laid down their lives, gladly, for their children, that the daughters of these enslaved women had thought their greatest blessing from "Freedom" was that it meant they could keep their own children. And what had Meridian Hill done with *her* precious child? She had given him away. She thought of her mother as being worthy of this maternal history, and of herself as belonging to an unworthy minority, for which there was no precedent and of which she was, as far as she knew, the only member.

After she had figuratively kissed the ground of the campus and walked about its lawns intent on bettering herself, she knew for certain she had broken something, for she began hearing a voice when she studied for exams, and when she walked about the academic halls, and when she looked from her third-floor dormitory window. A voice that cursed her existence—an existence that could not live up to the standard of motherhood that had gone before. It said, over and over, until she would literally reel in the streets, her head between her hands: Why don't you die? Why not kill yourself? Jump into the traffic! Lie down under the wheels of that big truck! Jump off the roof, as long as you're up there! Always, the voice. Mocking, making fun. It frightened her because the voice urging her on—the voice that said terrible things about her lack of value—was her own voice. It was talking to her, and it was full of hate.

Her teachers worked her hard, her first year at Saxon. She read night and day, making up for lost time. But no matter how hard she labored she was always willing to tackle more, because she knew almost no one there, and because Saxon was a peaceful but strange, still, place to her, and because she was grateful to be distracted. She was not to pause long enough to respond to this spiritual degeneration in herself until she was in her second year.

The Driven Snow

We are as chaste and pure as
the driven snow.
We watch our manners, speech
and dress just so;
And in our heads we carry our
greatest fame
That we are blessed to perpetuate
the Saxon name!

She *had* felt blessed her first year at Saxon. It was so beautiful! The tall red brick towers, the old courtyards, the giant trees—especially the greatest tree of them all, The Sojourner. This tree filled her with the same sense of minuteness and hugeness, of past and present, of sorrow and ecstasy that she had known at the Sacred Serpent. It gave her a profound sense of peace (which was only possible when she could feel invisible) to know slaves had found shelter in its branches. When her spirits were low, as they were often enough that first year, she would sit underneath The Sojourner and draw comfort from her age, her endurance, the stories the years told of her, and her enormous size. When she sat beneath The Sojourner, she knew she was not alone.

She was happy to make friends with Anne-Marion Coles, who seemed to her as sharp and bright as a blade of sunlight. It was Anne-Marion who had balked at singing the school song as it was written and who created instead the "parallel song," the beginning of which was: "We are as choice and prime as the daily steak." Naturally, steak was a food they never had at Saxon. They sang it with gusto while their classmates sang tamely of being like driven snow.

Of course it was kept secret from everyone that Meridian had been married and divorced and had had a child. It was assumed that Saxon young ladies were, by definition, virgins. They were treated always as if they were thirteen years old. This included the imposition on the student body of a requirement that was particularly awkward for Meridian that had to do with religion: Each morning at eight all Saxon students were required to attend a chapel service at which one girl was expected to get up on the platform and tell—in a ten-minute speech—of some way in which she had resisted evil and come out on the right side of God. Meridian could not recall any temptation that she had resisted, and whether she had resisted temptation or not, she did not believe she now stood even in the vicinity of God. In fact, Meridian was not sure there was a God, and when her turn came, she said so. She was still a very naive country girl who had expected an atmosphere in college that was different from that in her local church. She was wrong. When her fellow students found themselves near her afterward they would look about as if they expected lightning to strike, and her teachers let her know she was a willful, sinful girl.

She began to have headaches that were so severe they caused her to stutter when she spoke. She dreamed of such horrible things she would wake up shaking. Still, when she thought of the extraordinary opportunity she had in attending Saxon College, which had an excellent social and academic reputation, she knew herself to be extremely fortunate. She studied hard and made the dean's list, and during her second year she joined the Atlanta Movement. She found it impossible to study while others were being beaten and jailed. It was also, surprisingly, an escape for her. After her friendship with Anne-Marion, they marched often together and would go to jail with their toothbrushes and books and cigarettes under their arms. In jail they were allowed to smoke, which helped to calm their shrieking nerves. On Saxon campus itself, ironically, smoking led to expulsion, as did any other form of "decadent" behavior.

The emphasis at Saxon was on form, and the preferred "form" was that of the finishing school girl whose goal, wherever she would later find herself in the world, was to be *accepted* as an equal because she knew and practiced all the proper social rules. The administration of the college neither condoned Saxon students' participation in the Atlanta

Movement nor discouraged it. Once it was understood that the students could not be stopped, their involvement, as much as possible, was ignored. All of Saxon's rules, against smoking, drinking, speaking loudly, going off campus without an escort, remaining off campus after six, talking to boys before visiting hours, remained in effect. It was understood that a student who allowed herself to be arrested did so at her own academic risk. Fortunately, there were teachers who would lie for the students—a week in jail became a week on a field trip and was certainly as informative for the student as any field trip could ever be—though everyone knew this was a lie. Or a teacher might himself end up in jail. That too was ignored, though his name and photograph appeared in the papers.

A saying about Saxon was that you could do anything there, as long as you wore spotless white gloves. But because the gloves must remain clean and white, there was very little you could do. In fact, Meridian and the other students felt they had two enemies: Saxon, which wanted them to become something—ladies—that was already obsolete, and the larger, more deadly enemy, white racist society. It was not unusual for students to break down under the pressures caused by the two. One of Meridian's classmates, a gentle drama student from Ohio, had been dragged out of a picket line by four thugs and forced, on the main street in Atlanta, to drink a pint of ammonia. Later, after she had recovered physically, in the infirmary, though was obviously far from recovered mentally, she was severely chastised one evening for standing about in the bushes near her dorm with her boyfriend. Neither of them had noticed that calling hours had ended ten minutes earlier. The girl's nerves were wrecked, and she was forced to withdraw from school for the rest of the term.

Meridian, the former wife and mother, already felt herself to be flying under false colors as an "innocent" Saxon student. The scenes she personally witnessed in the Atlanta streets, combined with this, caused the majority of her waking moments to seem fragmented, surreal. She saw small black children, with short, flashing black legs, being chased by grown white men brandishing ax handles. She saw old women dragged out of stores and beaten on the sidewalk, their humility of a lifetime doing them no good. She saw young black men of great spiritual beauty changed overnight into men who valued nothing.

Things happened. One day, along with a group of demonstrators headed for downtown Atlanta, Meridian passed a young girl, nubile, pretty, with long brown pigtails, sitting on the steps of her house, waving. On impulse Meridian called to her: "Come join us," she cried. The girl, pigtails flying, came. Once downtown they sat in at a luncheon counter in Woolworth's and, after being doused with catsup, smeared with mustard and sprinkled with salt and pepper by white patrons of the store, they were arrested. Meridian had tried to keep the girl, whose name was Anne, with her, but in the confusion she disappeared. In the middle of the night there were screams from another cell, far down the row. Screams, according to the guards, of an alcoholic who thought she was being chased around her cell by giant spiders. But Meridian knew it was Anne, and though she never saw her again, she began to imagine she did, and the screams became an accompaniment to the guilt already weighing her down.

Meridian found, when she was not preoccupied with the Movement, that her thoughts turned with regularity and intensity to her mother, on whose account she endured wave after wave of an almost primeval guilt. She imagined her mother in church, in which she had invested all that was still energetic in her life, praying for her daughter's soul, and yet, having no concern, no understanding of her daughter's *life* whatsoever; but Meridian did not condemn her for this. Away from her mother, Meridian thought of her as Black Motherhood personified, and of that great institution she was in terrible awe, comprehending as she did the horror, the narrowing of perspective, for mother and for child, it had invariably meant.

Meridian felt as if her body, growing frailer every day under the stress of her daily life, stood in the way of a reconciliation between her mother and that part of her own soul her mother could, perhaps, love. She valued her body less, attended to it less, because she hated its obstruction.

Only during a crisis could she forget. While other students dreaded confrontation with police she welcomed it, and was capable of an inner gaiety, a sense of freedom, as she saw the clubs slashing down on her from above. Only once was she beaten into unconsciousness, and it was not the damage done to her body that she remembered when she woke up, but her feeling of yearning, of heartsick longing for forgiveness, as she saw the bright lights explode behind the red blood that curtained her face, and her feeling of hope as the harsh light of consciousness began to fade.

After The Wild Child's death she could not live on campus, although she continued to attend classes, and lived instead in the ghetto that surrounded it. It was a poor community but friendly and very clean. In order to pay her rent and to buy other items that one needed at a school like Saxon—tennis racket, bathing suit, ballet slippers and tights, etc.—she went to work as a typist for a professor who had recently retired and whose office was a few blocks from her door. He was a very old man who had, years ago, known her mother's family. It was her mother who encouraged her to take the job, reminding her that her father could not afford to send Meridian the two or three dollars a week she had asked him to send. His health was poor, and with the loss of the farm he was diminished in every way. He was no longer qualified to teach, now that integration was threatening the schools, and was doing odd jobs when and where he could find them.

It was her mother who first noticed that Meridian's thick, shoulder-length hair was beginning to thin. She even essayed a joke about how Meridian should be careful not to wind up bald, like Nelda's mother. It did not surprise Meridian that her hair came out as she combed it, any more than it surprised her that her vision sometimes blurred. She was too driven to notice; and it seemed essential to her then that whatever happened to her she should be prepared to accept. Besides, she was in love, with Truman.

The Conquering Prince

Truman stood on the other side of the screen door in a flowing Ethiopian robe of extravagantly embroidered white, his brown eyes aglow with excitement. Everyone thought him handsome because his nose was so keen and his skin was tan and not black; and Meridian, though disliking herself for it, thought him handsome for exactly those reasons, too. Or had, until, when she had known him for about a year, she began to look closely at him. With scrutiny, much of the handsomeness disappeared behind the vain, pretentious person Truman was. And his teeth were far from good.

But the sly, serious double takes were still in the future. Therefore, she threw open the door for him with such passionate force it banged like a shot against the wall. Truman strode in like a conquering prince returning to his lands.

"You look fantastic!" Meridian breathed, as she cuddled up in his arms.

"Et toi aussi," he replied in French. *"Tu es très magnifique!"*

Truman loved all the foreign cultures of the

world, but his favorite was French. He had spent a year in Avignon and Paris. He believed profoundly that anything said in French sounded better, and he also believed that people who spoke French were better than people *(les pauvres, les misérables!)* who did not.

Therefore, *"Bon!"* said Meridian—which was the only French expression with which she felt comfortable. Luckily, she understood the language better than she spoke it, because Truman would continue to speak it throughout the evening. When he talked to her she had to translate every syllable into English before answering. Their conversation moved slowly. But it didn't matter. She loved being with Truman. She felt protected when she was with him. To her he was courageous and "new." He was, in any case, unlike any other black man she had known. He was a man who fought against obstacles, a man who could become anything, a man whose very words were unintelligible without considerable thought. She also wanted to make hot, quick, mindless love with him whenever he was near. When he touched her now, on the arms where they joined her shoulders, she trembled against him, faint with desire, as the description read in old novels. She had never felt faint with desire before and felt she had discovered a missing sense.

"I am so glad you came to Saxon," he whispered, *en français*, of course. "You were going to waste out there in the sticks. Speaking of which," he suddenly said, drawing back, but keeping his arms tight about her, "aren't you losing weight?"

She buried her nose in the center of his throat and sucked his collarbone. They were going to a party, but if he didn't stop caressing her shoulders, whispering in French (which did sound awfully sexy) and looking at her with his wild brown eyes, she knew they would never make it. So she said, "Let's go," abruptly, pushing him reluctantly but firmly from her, and preceded him out the door.

Driving through town Meridian told him of the three white exchange students who had come on the march with them that afternoon.

"From where?" Truman asked. "Swarthmore?"

"No, Smith and Carleton."

"What do they look like?"

"One is exactly like the little Dutch boy on Dutch Boy paints. A pale blonde with ear-length hair. She's the prettiest. The other two are kind of homely. Susan is short and mousy with thick legs. Lynne is thin and dark, with bright black eyes that sort of stab at you. They've been here a week, and I've already been out canvassing voters with Lynne. I like her. She can't say 'saw,' she says, 'I *sarh* it.' And she starts her sentences with 'So.' Listen, let me tell you about this one lady's house we went to . . . way back in the sticks, on the edge of nowhere. This lady was sitting on her front porch, just as serene and untroubled as she could be. We should've seen that her Kingdom had already begun to approach, just by looking at her face. But we have to try everybody, right? She was one of these large, motherly types, with the tits, you know? Everybody's grandmother. Her food was cooking back somewhere on the stove. Butter beans, Lynne swore she could tell by the smell. Anyhow, we walked up and Lynne put one foot up on the lady's step. Her stomach was growling and she held her canvassing pad in front of it. The lady looked at her foot for a full minute.

" 'How y'all durin'?' she asked, and started fanning herself real slow, with one of those fans that show Jesus walking on water.

"Lynne said, 'My name is Lynne Rabinowitz . . .'

" 'LynnWizz,' the lady repeated.

" 'Yes, ma'am,' said Lynne.

" 'And who you down there uprootin' my collards with yo' eyes?'

" 'Meridian Hill,' I said, starting to laugh, because I liked her and because I sure was eyeball deep in her greens. They were so healthy they flashed in the sun, like they'd been greased.

" 'We came up here to ask you to register to vote.'

" 'Did?' asked the woman.

"Lynne's stomach let out a massive growl. 'You're not already registered, are you?' she asked, clutching her pad.

" 'Nome,' said the woman.

" 'You are Mrs. Mabel Turner, aren't you?' asked Lynne. She knew she was but she had to work that 'Mrs.' in somewhere.

"The slow fanning stopped. The light of recognition beamed from Mrs. Turner's eyes. 'Y'all must be them outside 'taters. Jooz an runnin' dogs. Y'all hongry?' She heaved herself up from her chair and started for the kitchen.

"We sat down at the table and had a big meal. Butter beans, collards, cornbread, the works. Mrs. Turner urged second helpings.

" 'So isn't this terrific? I'm about to pop right open,' said Lynne.

" 'If you did it wouldn't make much mess, skinny as you is,' said Mrs. Turner. 'I wants to feed y'all real good, 'cause I don't believe in votin'. The good Lord He take care of most of my problems. You know he heal the sick and race the dead. Comfort the uncomfortable and blesses the meek.'

"I said right then, 'We thank you for feeding us, Mrs. Turner,' and I got up to go, but Lynne wanted to argue.

" 'So God fixes the road in front of your house, does he?' she asked, using her Northern logic.

" 'Let's go,' I said. But no, she was just tuning up.

" 'Jesus Christ must be pleased to let you live in a house like this. The good Lord must get his jollies every time you have to hop outside to that toilet in the rain. The Holy Ghost must rejoice when your children catch pneumonia every winter. . . .'

" 'You sounds just like a blasphemer to me,' said Mrs. Turner. 'You sound like maybe you *is* kin to Judas Iscariot.' She frowned sadly and shook her head.

"Well, they argued and argued, until Mrs. Turner was afraid she had insulted her religion by feeding us. And Lynne refused to acknowledge the state of grace Mrs. Turner thought she was in.

" 'If only we hadn't *eaten*,' she kept saying, 'if

only we had refused the food, don't you think Mrs. Turner would have registered to vote?'

"Of course I said no. A blind man could have seen Mrs. Turner was just well beyond the boundaries of politics. . . ."

"*La fanatique*," said Truman.

Meridian drew back as if to strike him. "Stop talking like that about your cousins and aunts!"

Truman laughed. "And grandmother and so forth. . . . What's the name of the Dutch Boy?"

"Jill."

"C'est vrai?"

"Oui."

Meridian lit a cigarette and passed it to Truman. "I think they'll all be at the party tonight. They're eager to see how the natives make out after dark. Oka-mo-gah! Do you know what Charlene told me? She said that Jill was taking photographs of the girls straightening their hair and also of them coming out of the shower."

"Et puis?"

"Well, and then Charlene and the other girl whose pictures were being taken threatened to beat her up unless she destroyed the film. 'This here ain't New Guinea,' Charlene says she said."

"They were just curious about *les noirs*," said Truman. "When I was in Paris I was curious about the French. I'm sure I did strange things, too."

"Like photographing them while they styled their hair and when they emerged from the shower? Or is it true that the French never bathe?"

Truman laughed. "My little kitten has sharp

claws. Still," he said, "it pays to have a little tolerance with other people's curiosity. It never bothers me any more when foreigners look at my hair and say, 'A leetle beet of zee tar brush, eh?' "

"Everyone is proud to acknowledge a tiny bit of a 'bad' thing," said Meridian. "They know how fascinating it makes them."

She looked out the car window and realized they had stopped a few houses down from where the party was. Truman reached for her and gathered her tightly into his arms. She felt his tongue licking the au de cologne off her earlobes. His hands were squeezing the nipples of her breasts. When she pulled her head away he buried his face in her lap, an action that briefly shocked her. She felt warm tingling sensations creeping up from the bottom of her stomach.

"Let's not go to the party," he pleaded. "Let's go back to the apartment. Everybody else is here, we'll be alone. I want you."

"I love you," she said.

"And we're going to the party, right?" Truman sat up and ran his fingers through his hair.

"But do you understand?" Meridian asked. "I'm not a prude. Afraid, yes, but not a prude. One day soon we'll be together."

"You're so young," said Truman, getting out and adjusting his robe. "I wish I could make you feel how beautiful it would be with me."

"I feel it, I feel it!" cried Meridian, taking his hand and walking up the street.

At the party Meridian danced, as seemed to be

her fate at most parties, with a plodding young man from Arkansas. His first name was Terence; she deliberately kept herself innocent of his last. They pushed along the floor until a white boy broke in. Terence, exhibiting his freedom from prejudice, practically shoved Meridian into his arms.

"You go to school around here?" the white boy asked.

"Yes," said Meridian, "more or less." He was a head taller than she and her chin, when she looked up at him, poked into his chest. He was not ugly, only plucked-looking, with short black hair, shaved down around the bottom of his hairline, and teeth that had tiny white spots in the enamel, as if tiny pieces of seashell had been embedded there.

"Where are you from?" she asked. She hated to think in clichés at a time like this, when she could see he was gazing at her admiringly, but his dance was *very* stiff.

"Connecticut," he said. "We came down from the University of Connecticut. Con U," he added, and laughed. Meridian did not get the joke. She almost asked, "What you want to con me for, already?"

Someone had put a fast record on and they plunged about the room crazily. When they stopped to breathe Meridian looked about for Truman.

"I'm looking for my date," she explained to Con U, who was following the sweep her eyes made across the room, unable to conceal his anxiety that she might walk away.

"Isn't that him over there?" asked Con U, delight in his voice.

Truman was sitting on the stairs that led up from the basement. The Dutch Boy was sitting cross-legged on the floor beneath him, looking up at him with—admiration? curiosity? hunger? Meridian was not sure. That the girl's skirt was above her knees she could see.

Con U laughed. "Looks like he's doing all right for himself," and he sort of hunkered over her, his elbow against the wall. He seemed to her peculiarly rustic, and though now that she was in college she prided herself on having catholic tastes when it came to men, white farmers were not yet included.

"My name is Scott," he said, "after Scott Fitzgerald. My mother loves his books."

"Ummm . . ." said Meridian, grudgingly relinquishing her own name.

He was also going to be a talker.

Did she go to dances often? Did she like to dance? How far away was her home town? Did her mother like to dance? What kind of work did her father do? Did *he* like to dance? And what of the school—did she like it? Did they teach dancing there? And of the demonstrations—how many had she gone on? Did she believe, truly, that one ought to protest in this way? Wasn't there some other method that might work and prove less disastrous than marching in the street? Didn't our Constitution provide for just such emergencies as the present racial crisis? What did she think of the Constitution? the founding fathers? He wondered if they would like what was going on in the country? Did *they* believe in unlawful protest? He thought it was an interesting question. Wonder, come to think of it, how they passed their time when not drafting the Constitution? Did *they* dance?

"Terence," she called, clutching his shoulder as he plodded by, "I'm so glad you've come back. You know I promised you the last dance."

She looked about for Truman to rescue her but he was nowhere in sight.

Terence beamed with pride and joy. Off they moved to a dreary finish.

"I went out for cigarettes." said Truman, adjusting his robe. Meridian stood on the porch. Everyone else had left. Fearing the kindled gleam in Terence's eye and not feeling up to a struggle, she'd waited for Truman.

"God, you just don't know what a drag this evening was," said Meridian, who was too tired not to complain.

When they reached her house she invited him in, but he too was feeling tired and sleepy.

"Maybe tomorrow night," he said, stifling a yawn.

But she did not see Truman again, alone (except for one heart-breaking time), for several months, not until he had read *The Souls of Black Folk*, in fact. The exchange students, all three of them, had gone back North then, and he needed someone to discuss Du Bois with. "The man was a *genius!*" he cried, and he read passages from the book that he said were reflective of his and Meridian's souls. But

Meridian was reading F. Scott Fitzgerald then, though she never gave up any of the Du Bois she already knew. It just seemed too deep for conversation with Truman, somehow. He was startled by the coolness with which she received his assertion that what he had decided, after reading *"le maitre,"* was that if he dated white girls it must be, essentially, a matter of sex. She laughed when she saw he expected her to be pleased and reassured, a bitter laugh that sent him away again, his chin thrust forward against her misunderstanding.

The time she had seen Truman, after he began dating the exchange students, had been bitterly regretted. And for her part in what happened, Meridian paid dearly.

She had been walking down the street from her job at the old professor's and—walking with her head down—had not seen Truman coming toward her. They almost passed each other before he stopped and turned, his brown eyes very dark and hot against the green polo shirt he wore.

"Meridian?"

"Hi," she said, feeling embarrassed to see him now that he was busy dating the exchange students. It was strange and unfair, but the fact that he dated them—and so obviously because their color made them interesting—made *her* ashamed, as if she were less.

He came up to her and casually placed his arm around her shoulders. "You walk with your head down. It should be up. Proud and free." And he chucked her playfully under the chin.

She looked at him wondering if he had, as she had done, marched that day. As a rule, he said, he didn't march any more, "because what I believe cannot be placed on a placard." And she had teased him about that and said, "How about just the words 'Freedom, Liberty, Equality'? That would cover what you believe in, wouldn't it?" She was also tempted to add white exchange students. But how polite she was! How bewildered by his preference. It went against everything she had been taught to expect.

For she realized what she *had* been taught was that nobody wanted white girls except their empty-headed, effeminate counterparts—white boys—whom her mother assured her smelled (in the mouth) of boiled corn and (in the body) of thirty-nine-cent glue. As far back as she could remember it seemed something *understood:* that while white men would climb on black women old enough to be their mothers—"for the experience"—white women were considered sexless, contemptible and ridiculous by all. They did not even smell like glue or boiled corn; they smelled of nothing since they did not sweat. They were clear, dead water.

Her mother, though not a maid, had often worked for white families near Christmastime in order to earn extra money, and she told her family—in hushed, carefully controlled language, keeping her face set over her ironing board—about the lusty young sons home from school for the holidays, calling her by her first name, of course, and begging and pleading and even (and her mother scoffed) getting all blubbery the way white men get. "Gertrude pul-eze," her mother mocked the slow pull of the pseudocultivated Southern gentleman. "What are you talkin' 'bout, *Mr.* So-an-so?" (This to a twenty-one-year-old kid, her anger and her religion choking her.) "I'm old enough to be your grandma. I can remember when your mama was a girl. You wouldn't hang around any of your mama's friends like this. Why you botherin' me?"

This would lead Mrs. Hill directly into an exhortation on her religious as opposed to her human dignity. (Because she rightly assumed "Mr. So-an-so" would not be interested in the latter.) She was black, wasn't she? And a female. (Not lady, not even woman, since both these words conjured up something larger than sex; they spoke of a somebody as opposed to a something.) Yes, it was understood about white men. Some of them liked black women for sex and said so. For the others it was a matter of gaining experience, initiation into the adult world. The maid, the cook, a stray child, anything not too old or repulsive would do. In Mrs. Hill's voice there was a well, a reservoir, an ocean of disgust. And when she described white men it was with weary religion-restrained hatred. She could speak freely because the general opinion of white men, among blacks, was in her favor. She spoke of their faces as if they were the faces of moose, of oxen, of wet, slobbery walruses. Besides, she said, they were manipulated by their wives, which did not encourage respect.

But what had her mother said about white women? She could actually remember very little, but her impression had been that they were frivolous, helpless creatures, lazy and without ingenuity. Occasionally one would rise to the level of bitchery, and this one would be carefully set aside when the collective "others" were discussed. Her grandmother—an erect former maid who was now a midwife—held strong opinions, which she expressed in this way: 1. She had never known a white woman she liked after the age of twelve. 2. White women were useless except as baby machines which would continue to produce little white people who would grow up to oppress her. 3. Without servants all of them would live in pigsties.

Who would dream, in her home town, of kissing a white girl? Who would want to? What were they good for? What did they do? They only seemed to hang about laughing, after school, until when they were sixteen or seventeen they got married. Their pictures appeared in the society column, you saw them pregnant a couple of times. Then you were no longer able to recognize them as girls you once "knew." They sank into a permanent oblivion. One never heard of them *doing* anything that was interesting. Oh, one might escape to join the WAC's. Quite a few—three or four a year, the homely ones—attended a college in the state (which kept the local library and English departments supplied) but there were positively no adventurers—unless you counted the alcoholics—among them. If one of them did manage to experiment with life to the extent that the process embarrassed her parents (or her parents' friends, the folks at home who filled the churches every Sunday) it was never found out by anyone in the black community.

On the other hand, black women were always imitating Harriet Tubman—escaping to become something unheard of. Outrageous. One of her sister's friends had become, somehow, a sergeant in the army and knew everything there was to know about enemy installations and radio equipment. A couple of girls her brothers knew had gone away broke and come back, years later, as a doctor and a schoolteacher. Two other girls went away married to men and returned home married to each other. This perked up the community. Tongues wagged. But in the end the couple enjoyed visiting their parents, old friends, and were enjoyed in turn. "How do you suppose they do it?" was a question which—though of course not printed in the newspaper—still made all the rounds. But even in more conventional things, black women struck out for the unknown. They left home scared, poor black girls and came back (some of them) successful secretaries and typists (this had seemed amazing to everyone, that there should be firms in Atlanta and other large cities that would *hire* black secretaries). They returned, their hair bleached auburn or streaked with silver, or perhaps they wore a wig. It would be bold, deathly straight or slightly curled, and remind everyone of the Italians—like Pier Angeli—one saw in the movies. Their pocketbooks, their shoes, would *shine*, and their faces (old remembered faces now completely reconstructed by Max Factor and Maybelline) perfected masks through which the voice of some person formerly known came through.

Then there were simply the good-time girls who came home full of bawdy stories of their exploits in the big city; one watched them seduce the local men with dazzling ease, some who used to be lovers and might be still. In their cheap, loud clothing, their newly repaired teeth, their flashy cars, their too-gold shimmering watches and pendants—they were still a success. They commanded attention. They deserved admiration. Only the rejects—not of men, but of experience, adventure—fell into the domestic morass that even the most intelligent white girls appeared to be destined for. There seemed nothing about white women that was enviable. Perhaps one might covet a length of hair, if it swung long and particularly fine. But that was all. And hair was dead matter that continued—only if oiled—to shine.

Of course Meridian appropriated all the good qualities of black women to herself, now that she was awake enough to be aware of them. In her life with Eddie she knew she had lacked courage, lacked initiative or a mind of her own. And yet, from somewhere, had come the *will* that had got her to Saxon College. At times she thought of herself as an adventurer. It thrilled her to think she belonged to the people who produced Harriet Tubman, the only American woman who'd led troops in battle.

But Truman, alas, did not want a general beside him. He did not want a woman who tried, however encumbered by guilts and fears and remorse, to claim her own life. She knew Truman would have liked her better as she had been as Eddie's wife, for all that he admired the flash of her face across a picket line—an attractive woman, but asleep.

But now, as they walked under the trees along the campus paths and the chimes from the campus clock rang out their inappropriate eighteenth-century melodies, she needed his arm around her shoulders. The truth was, she had missed him and regretted every single time she had turned him down.

When they got to her apartment she was thankful that he walked in behind her.

"What did he give you this time?" Truman asked.

"Some raisins, Fig Newtons, a carton of Cokes," she said, swinging them up on the table, "and enough money to buy a *good* tennis racket."

"He sure must want a daughter," said Truman, opening a Coke and drinking it in long swallows. "Unless," he said, and grinned at her, "*unless* he's a sugar daddy." He burst out laughing at the thought. "Does he ever," he asked, his eyes twinkling, "hobble you around his desk?"

Meridian put the remainder of the Cokes into the refrigerator. She did not smile, until the silence caused her to consider what Truman said, then her lips briefly twitched. "Nope," she said quickly. "The thought of some live action would stew his old heart to death."

But of course that was not true. The truth was, she *was* chased around the desk by Mr. Raymonds.

The truth was, her scholarship did not cover all her school expenses and her other needs, too. The truth *was* she depended on the extras Mr. Raymonds gave her. Every Coke, every cookie, every can of deviled ham, every tennis racket that he gave her meant one less that she had to buy.

Yes, Mr. Raymonds did *limp* her around his desk. And what was more, and worse, he caught her. But she knew Truman would never understand. She had hardly understood or believed it herself, at first. The first time Mr. Raymonds accidentally brushed against her, she thought she'd imagined it. After all, he was somebody important, a university professor, covered with honors (his walls were, anyway). They fairly sagged with the plaques nailed there (and she was not sophisticated enough yet to find them tacky) saying he had been 1. Head of the Colored YMCA from 1919–1925; 2. An Elder in the Episcopalian Church; 3. The Masonic Temple's Man of the Year 1935–36; 4. Best Teacher of Farming Methods 1938–39. He had written books on various aspects of farming and was an expert. When he gave her copies of his books, autographed, she was as thrilled as anything, and quickly mailed them home to her father. He gave her the books her first day on the job.

He did not tell her anything about his wife, but she had seen a picture of her once, a sourfaced woman, very dark, as were the women often chosen by very light-skinned black men. She had noticed that it went either this way, with lightcolored men, or the other. There didn't seem to be a middle ground. In Mr. Raymonds' case, he had probably chosen a dark-skinned wife because he was one of those old-fashioned "race men," the radical nationalists of his day—the 1920's. He loved to talk even now of The Race as if it were a lump of homogenized matter that could be placed this way or that way, at will, to effect change.

Mr. Raymonds stuck up for the race as a whole, although Meridian thought she detected a slightly defensive attitude around younger and darker-skinned men. It was as if he had to prove himself. He was also very emotional about protecting the virtue of black women from white men. Once he had seen her talking to a white divinity student on the corner before turning in to his building to work, and he had been red in the face from anger. Before she went home she had been told exactly how many black women had reported rape at the hands of white men in the years between 1896 and 1963. She assumed he made up the figure, but she gasped anyway. The divinity student, ironically, had been from South Africa, and she had spoken to him out of a kind of perverse curiosity. She thought because she was black she would notice some kind of strain come into his face, but there was nothing at all. She might have been as white and as near divinity as he.

This curiosity was the way she was, sometimes, with whites. Mostly they did not seem quite real to her. They seemed very stupid the way they attempted to beat down everybody in their path and then know nothing about it. She saw them sometimes as hordes of elephants, crushing everything underfoot, stolid and heavy and yet—unlike the elephant—forgetting.

Mr. Raymonds was tall and bony and the color of caramel candy that is being stretched, with short white hair and a drooping left eyelid. She hated his teeth; they were all false or mostly false, and held together with wires that would have glittered if he ever cleaned his mouth. He never did. Consequently his teeth seemed to be covered with yellowish flannel and the smell of his breath was nauseating, as if his whole mouth were a tunnel of sewerage. He had not always been thin. And even now he was more bony than thin. As a young man he had been heavily muscled. He grew gaunt with age. When he grabbed her as she stepped warily into his office and attempted to rub his old penis against her, she felt nothing but his hard pelvic bones poking her in the stomach.

He wanted her to sit on his lap, which she would sometimes do. Then he would open up his desk drawer and pull out the goodies he bought for her. Tins of tuna, bags of mints and Baby Ruths, dimestore combs and even, sometimes, typing paper. He nestled his long nose in her hair or as far under her chin as she would let him, all the while squirming under her so that some of the desperate delight he was experiencing would work its way up into his limp penis. He had no luck that she could ever tell.

Each day when she rose to go—having typed letters for him in a veritable swamp fog of bad breath—he clasped her in his arms, dragging her away from the door, the long bones of his thighs forcing her legs apart, attempting to force her to the floor. But she smiled and struggled and struggled and smiled, and pretended she knew nothing of his intentions—a thought which no doubt aroused him all the more. As she twisted and squirmed, keeping her face averted as much as possible from his lips and his breath, his face became gray with determination and sweat, his breathing became hoarse and labored, and when he looked at her the gleam in his eye was pathetic.

"What's the matter?" asked Truman.

"Nothing," she said quickly. "Tell me what's really been happening?"

"I've been working out at the country club again," he said, sighing and lying back on the sofa. "God, I hate those bastards. You just don't know how hard a time I have making a little bread." He reached out and caught her wrist, pulling her down to the couch. "Those crackers throw cigarettes in the pool for the express purpose of making me pick them out. And I can't wait until tomorrow either. Oh no. 'Trooo-munn,' some old shit calls, 'go git them butts out the pool before some more of our guests arrive.' And while I'm fishing for butts some of their old skinny broads saunter over to watch and of course to give advice. 'Trooo-munn,' they coo, 'I bleve you got to lean over more this way, don't you?' Or, 'You're just a very ajul boy, for a boy your size.' And I have to just stand there and grin and bear it. I despise them," he said vehemently, socking a pillow, his other hand tight around her arm. "You women sure are lucky not to have to be up against'em all the time."

The short muttering laugh that answered him was black with derision, and Truman looked at Meridian sharply.

"You're right," he said, "we don't have to talk about shit like that tonight. Come here, woman, I missed you."

She could not help remarking how his own sense of masculinity gratified him. The pressure around her wrist, like his crude order, was certainly not necessary, since she was already lying, like a beached fish, across his lap.

With his warm long fingers he stroked the insides of her arms, then kissed her on the lips. Her mind was still working perfectly. She had planned, because of the exchange students, to be unmoved, but something alive seemed to be moving, unfolding, spreading and reaching out in the bottom of her stomach. Indeed, she felt, and carefully noted it, as if the entire center of her body was beginning to melt. She decided to click her mind off, and her body seemed to move into his of its own accord. Deliberately though, when he began to suck her nipples through her blouse, she sat up and took it off. He fastened his mouth on one nipple and his fingers pinched and stroked the other.

The exchange students were banished to a corner of the world her thoughts did not need to follow. She chased them there with an imaginary broom, invented special for that purpose. It was a long black broom with a yellow ribbon around its handle. In her hands it scoured both heaven and earth until only the two of them were left. Truman hesitated when his hand touched her panties. She rose up, silently, and let her skirt, bra and panties drop to the floor. Her gaze fell on his penis. It seemed to her extremely large and oddly curving, as if distorted by its own arrogant weight. When she took it in her hand Truman shivered, his face contorted. His face moved her. She guided him into her and they fucked (she consciously thought of it as that), they fucked, it seemed, for hours, and over and over again she nearly reached a climax only to lose it. Finally, when she was weary enough to scream, Truman came and quickly fell asleep. He mumbled she was very sexy as he turned. It was only then that she remembered he had not worn a condom—the only means of contraception she knew.

Flinging his leg off her (he had slept with the curve of his foot locked about her ankle) she hurried to the bathroom and strained over the commode. She wished she had had a douche bag. Instead she took a glass of hot water and worked some of the water up her while lying in the tub. She had made up her mind before coming to Atlanta not to have sex. When she went back into the living room, Truman was gone.

He had gone back to the last of the exchange students, the one she had liked, Lynne Rabinowitz. It was for this reason, among others, that he never knew she was pregnant. On her way to have an abortion she saw them riding across campus in his father's new red car. From a distance, they both looked white to her, that day. Later, as the doctor tore into her body without giving her anesthesia (and while he lectured her on her morals) and she saw stars because of the pain, she was still seeing them laughing, carefree, together. It was not that she wanted him any more, she did not. It enraged her that she could be made to endure such pain, and that he was oblivious to it. She was also disgusted with the fecundity of her body that got pregnant on less screwing than anybody's she had ever heard of. It seemed doubly unfair that after all her sexual "experience" and after one baby and one abortion she had not once been completely fulfilled by sex.

Her doctor was the one from Saxon College, only now in private practice. "I could tie your tubes," he chopped out angrily, "if you'll let me in on some of all this extracurricular activity." His elbow somehow rested heavily on her navel and a whirling hot pain shot from her uterus to her toes. She felt sure she'd never walk again. She looked at him until his hard face began to blur. "Burn'em out by the roots for all I care." She had left his office wide-legged with blood soaking her super Kotex and cramps bending her double, but she was crying for other reasons.

Truman never knew. She thought about telling him, but when she considered he might have the nerve to pity her, she knew she would rather have bitten her tongue in half. After the exchange students left he strolled up to her one day as she emerged from one of her classes.

"You know," he said, squinting up his eyes as if seeing something clearly but with immense strain, "I don't know what was wrong with me. You're obviously a stone fox. I don't see why we had to break up."

"You're kidding?" She said this more to herself than to him. She felt nothing and was relieved. She wondered why, or rather how that term came to be so popular. Surely no one had bothered to analyze it as they said it. In her mind she carried a stone fox. It was heavy, gray and could not move.

"Aw, don't be like that," he said, stopping her on the walk and looking into her eyes. "I think I'm in love with you, African woman. Always have been. Since the first."

She laughed. It seemed only fair, and her mind was working perfectly after all. "You're kidding again?"

"We could be happy together. I *know* we could. I can make you come. I almost did it that time, didn't I?" He looked at her, waiting for her to stammer or blush. "All the time I thought you didn't like to fuck. You do, don't you? Anyway, your body is beautiful. So warm, so brown . . ."

She turned away, shame for him, for what he was revealing, making her sick.

"It's over. Let it stay."

But he looked at her with eyes of new discovery.

"You're *beautiful,*" he whispered worshipfully. Then he said, urgently, "*Have* my beautiful black babies."

And she drew back her green book bag and

began to hit him. She hit him three times before she even knew what was happening. Then she hit him again across the ear and a spiral from a tablet cut his cheek. Blood dripped onto his shirt. When she noticed the blood she turned and left him to the curiosity of the other students crowding there.

The Recurring Dream

She dreamed she was a character in a novel and that her existence presented an insoluble problem, one that would be solved only by her death at the end.

She dreamed she was a character in a novel and that her existence presented an insoluble problem, one that would be solved only by her death at the end.

She dreamed she was a character in a novel and that her existence presented an insoluble problem, one that would be solved only by her death at the end.

Even when she gave up reading novels that encouraged such a solution—and nearly all of them did—the dream did not cease.

She felt as if a small landslide had begun behind her brows, as if things there had started to slip. It was a physical feeling and she paid it no mind. She just began to take chances with her life. She would go alone to small towns where blacks were not welcome on the sidewalks after dark and she would stand waiting, watching the sun go down. She walked for miles up and down Atlanta streets until she was exhausted, without once paying any attention to the existence of cars. She began to forget to eat.

The day before her graduation from Saxon she suddenly noticed, as she looked at a rack of clean glasses in the dining room, that they were bathed in a bluish light. When she held up one hand in front of her face it seemed bluish also, as if washed in ink. Although Anne-Marion had moved in with her she did not mention the blue spells to her, and they would sit talking, eating the goodies she brought home from Mr. Raymonds and reading about Socialism.

Both girls had lived and studied enough to know they despised capitalism; they perceived it had done well in America because it had rested directly on their fathers' and mothers' backs. The difference between them was this: Anne-Marion did not know if she would be a success as a capitalist, while Meridian did not think she could enjoy owning things others could not have. Anne-Marion wanted black to have the same opportunity to make as much money as the richest white people. But Meridian wanted the destruction of the rich as a class and the eradication of all personal economic preserves. Her senior thesis was based on the notion that no one should be allowed to own more land than could be worked in a day, by hand. Anne-

Marion thought this was quaint. When black people can own the seashore, she said, I want miles and miles of it. And I never want to see a face I didn't invite walking across my sand. Meridian reminded her of her professed admiration for Socialist and Communist theories. Yes, Anne-Marion replied. I have the deepest admiration for them, but since I haven't had a chance to have a capitalist fling yet, the practice of those theories will have to wait awhile.

But Anne-Marion, Meridian would say, that is probably exactly what Henry Ford said! Tell Henry I agree with him, said Anne-Marion.

These exchanges would be marked by laughter and the attempt to pretend they were not serious.

Fuck Democracy, Anne-Marion would say, biting into a cookie. Fuck the Free World. Let the Republicans and the Democrats-as-we-know-them fuck each other's grandmothers.

Meridian would laugh and laugh, until her arms grew tired from slapping the side of her bed.

But one day the blue became black and she temporarily—for two days—lost her sight. Until then she had not thought seriously of going to a doctor. For one thing, she had no money. For another, if she went to the campus doctor he would want payment for having tied her tubes. Still, when she awoke from a long faint several days after her eyesight returned and found him standing over her, she was not surprised. His presence seemed appropriate. Without waiting to hear her symptoms he had her lifted up on the examining table—using his best officious manner before his nurses—and she was given a thorough and painful pelvic examination. Her breasts were routinely and exhaustively felt. She was asked if she slept with boys. She was asked why she slept with boys. Didn't she know that boys nowadays were no good and could get her into trouble?

He thought she'd better come to his off-campus office for further consultation; there, he said, he had more elaborate equipment with which to test her.

She returned to the apartment sicker than when she left. Happily, two days later, neither the fainting nor the blue-black spells had returned. Then she found—on trying to get out of bed—that her legs no longer worked. Since she had experienced paralysis before, this worried her less than the losing of her sight. As the days passed—and she attempted to nibble at the dishes Anne-Marion brought—she discovered herself becoming more and more full, with no appetite whatsoever. And, to her complete surprise and astonished joy, she began to experience ecstasy.

Sometimes, lying on her bed, not hungry, not cold, not worried (because she realized the worry part of her brain had been the landslide behind her brows and that it had slid down and therefore no longer functioned), she felt as if a warm, strong light bore her up and that she was a beloved part of the universe; that she was innocent even as the rocks are innocent, and unpolluted as the first waters. And when Anne-Marion sat beside the bed and scolded her for not eating, she was amazed that

Anne-Marion could not see how happy and content she was.

Anne-Marion was alarmed. Before her eyes, Meridian seemed to be slipping away. Still, the idea that Meridian might actually die, while smiling happily at a blank ceiling, seemed preposterous, and she did nothing about it. But one day, as she sat on her own bed across from Meridian's, reading a book of Marxist ideology that included *The Communist Manifesto,* which she considered a really thought-provoking piece of work, she glanced at Meridian's head in shock. For all around it was a full soft light, as if her head, the spikes of her natural, had learned to glow. The sight pricked an unconscious place in Anne-Marion's post-Baptist memory.

"Ah shit!" she said, stamping her foot, annoyed that she'd thought of Meridian in a religious context.

"What's the matter?" asked Meridian dreamily. She moved her head slightly and the soft bright light disappeared.

Anne-Marion hugged her book as if it were a lover going off on a long trip. "We've been raised wrong!" she said, "that's what's wrong." What she meant was, she no longer believed in God and did not like to think about Jesus (for whom she still felt a bitter, grudging admiration).

"How long has she been in bed?" asked Miss Winter.

"About a month," said Anne-Marion.

"You should have come to me sooner," said Miss Winter.

Miss Winter was also a misfit at Saxon College. Yellow, with bulging black eyes and an elaborate blue wig, she was the school's organist—one of only three black teachers on the faculty. The other two taught PE and French. It was she each morning who played the old English and German hymns the program required, and the music rose like marching souls toward the vaulted ceiling of the chapel. And yet, in her music class she deliberately rose against Saxon tradition to teach jazz (which she had learned somewhere in Europe to pronounce "jawhz") and spirituals and the blues (which she pronounced "blews"). It was thought each year that she would never survive to teach at Saxon the following one. But she endured. As aloof and ladylike as she appeared (and she never wore outfits the parts of which did not *precisely* match), her fights with the president and the college dean could be heard halfway across the campus.

Miss Winter was from Meridian's home town and had known Meridian's family all her life. She was a Saxon graduate herself, and when she learned Meridian had been accepted as a student she fought down her first feelings, which were base. She had enjoyed being the only person from her town to attend such a college; she did not wish to share this distinction. By the time Meridian arrived, however, she had successfully uprooted this feeling. She would not, even so, return the girl's timid greeting the first day they met.

She had once attended an oratorical competition at her old high school, where Meridian was well on her way to distinguishing herself. Meridian was reciting a speech that extolled the virtues of the Constitution and praised the superiority of The American Way of Life. The audience cared little for what she was saying, and of course they didn't believe any of it, but they were rapt, listening to her speak so passionately and with such sad valor in her eyes.

Then, in the middle of her speech, Meridian had seemed to forget. She stumbled and then was silent on the stage. The audience urged her on but she would not continue. Instead she covered her face with her hands and had to be led away.

Meridian's mother went out into the hallway where Meridian was and Miss Winter overheard them talking. Meridian was trying to explain to her mother that for the first time she really listened to what she was saying, knew she didn't believe it, and was so distracted by this revelation that she could not make the rest of her speech. Her mother. not listening to this explanation at all, or at least not attempting to understand it, was saying something else: She was reminding Meridian that whenever something went wrong for *her* she simply trusted in God, raised her head a little higher than it already was, stared down whatever was in her path, never looked back, and so forth.

Meridian, who was seated and whose eyes were red from crying, was looking up at her mother hopelessly. Standing over her, her mother appeared huge, a giant, a woman who *could* trust in God, hold up her head, never look back, and get through everything, whether she believed in it or not. Meridian, on the other hand, appeared smaller than she actually was and looked as though she wanted to melt into her seat. She had doubled over, as if she might shrink into a ball and disappear.

Miss Winter had pushed back the cuff of her gray mink coat and put a perfumed arm around Meridian's shoulders. She told her not to worry about the speech. "It's the same one they made me learn when I was here," she told her, "and it's no more true now than it was then." She had never said anything of the sort to anyone before and was surprised at how good it felt. A blade of green grass blew briefly across her vision and a fresh breeze followed it. She realized the weather was too warm for mink and took off her coat.

But Meridian continued to huddle there, and her mother, her body as stately as the prow of a ship, moved off down the hall where she stood head and shoulders above all the girls—Meridian's classmates—who seemed an insubstantial mass of billowing crinolines and flashy dresses, gathered there.

To Meridian, her mother *was* a giant. She had never perceived her in any other way. Or, if she did have occasional thoughts that challenged this conception she swept them out of her mind as petty and ridiculous. Even on the day Miss Winter remembered, Meridian's sadness had been only that she had failed her mother. That her mother was deliberately obtuse about what had happened meant nothing beside her own feelings of inadequacy and guilt. Besides, she had already forgiven her mother for anything she had ever done to her or might do, because to her, Mrs. Hill had persisted in bringing them all (the children, the husband, the family, the race) to a point far beyond where she, in her mother's place, her grandmother's place, her great-grandmother's place, would have stopped.

This was her mother's history as Meridian knew it:

Her mother's great-great-grandmother had been a slave whose two children were sold away from her when they were toddlers. For days she had followed the man who bought them until she was able to steal them back. The third time—after her owner had exhausted one of his field hands whipping her, and glints of bone began to show through the muscles on her back—she was allowed to keep them on the condition that they would eat no food she did not provide herself.

During the summers their existence was not so hard. They learned to pick berries at night, after the day's work in the fields, and they gathered poke salad and in the autumn lived on nuts they found in the woods. They smoked fish they caught in streams and the wild game she learned to trap. They were able to exist this way until the children were in their teens. Then their mother died, the result of years of slow starvation. The children were sold the day of their mother's burial.

Mrs. Hill's great-grandmother had been famous

for painting decorations on barns. She earned money for the man who owned her and was allowed to keep some for herself. With it she bought not only her own freedom, but that of her husband and children as well. In Meridian's grandmother's childhood, there were still barns scattered throughout the state that bloomed with figures her mother had painted. At the center of each tree or animal or bird she painted, there was somehow drawn in, so that it formed a part of the pattern, a small contorted face—whether of man or woman or child, no one could tell—that became her trademark.

Mrs. Hill's mother married a man of many admirable qualities. He was a person who kept his word, ran a prosperous farm and had a handsome face. But he also had no desire to raise children—though he enjoyed sex with any willing, good-looking woman who came his way—and he beat his wife and children with more pleasure than he beat his mules.

Mrs. Hill had spent the early part of her life scurrying out of her father's way. Later, when she was in her teens, she also learned to scurry out of the way of white men—because she was good-looking, defenseless and black. Her life, she told Meridian, was one of scurrying, and only one thing kept her going: her determination to be a schoolteacher.

The story of her pursuit of education was pitiful.

First, she had come up against her father, who said she did not need to go to school because if she only learned to cook collard greens, shortbread and fried okra, some poor soul of a man might have her, and second, she had to decide to accept the self-sacrifice of her mother, whom she had worshiped. Her mother, by that time, was pregnant with her twelfth child, and her hair had already turned white. But it was her mother who made the bargain with her father that allowed her to go to school. The agreement was wretched: School would cost twelve dollars a year, and her mother would have to earn every cent of it. Refusing to complain and, indeed, refusing even to discuss the hardship it would cause, her mother had gone out to do other people's laundry, and Meridian's mother remembered her trudging off—after doing her own washing and work in the fields—with her rub board under her arm.

Mrs. Hill had had only two pairs of cotton bloomers. She wore and washed, washed and wore. She had only one dress. She and her sister swapped dresses each day so they might have at least this much variety in their attire. They had gone without shoes much of the time. And yet, miraculously, Meridian's mother had finished school and, what was more, helped four of her sisters and brothers do the same. And she had become a schoolteacher, earning forty dollars a month, four months out of the year. (Her students were in the cotton fields the rest of the time.) She had bought her mother a coat and new pair of shoes with her first pay. Hers had also been the honor, a short time later, of paying for her mother's pink coffin.

When her mother talked about her childhood Meridian wept and clung to her hands, wishing with all her heart she had not been born to this already overburdened woman. Whatever smugness crept into her mother's voice—as when she said "I never stole, I was always clean, I never did wrong by anyone, I was never *bad;* I simply trusted in the Lord"—was unnoticed by her. It seemed to Meridian that her legacy from her mother's endurance, her unerring knowledge of rightness and her pursuit of it through all distractions, was one she would never be able to match. It never occurred to her that her mother's and her grandmother's extreme purity of life was compelled by necessity. They had not lived in an age of choice.

None of these thoughts could she convey to Miss Winter. She merely smiled at her from the calm plateau in her illness she had happily reached. Now and again she saw clouds drift across Miss Winter's head and she amused herself picking out faces that she knew. When she slept she dreamed she was on a ship with her mother, and her mother was holding her over the railing about to drop her into the sea. Danger was all around and her mother refused to let her go.

"Mama, I *love* you. Let me go," she whispered, licking the salt from her mother's black arms.

Instinctively, as if Meridian were her own child, Miss Winter answered, close to her ear on the pillow, "I forgive you."

The next morning Meridian ate all her breakfast, though it would not all stay down. For the first time she asked for a mirror and tried to sit up in bed. Soon, her strength exhausted, she slept. Anne-Marion watched the sun climb again to illuminate the edges of her hair, and knew she could not endure a friendship that required such caring vigilance. Meridian, for all her good intentions, might never be ready for the future, and that would be too painful. Anne-Marion could not continue to care about a person she could not save. Nor could she end a close friendship without turning on the friend.

One morning, when Meridian was standing by the window, her face pensive, nearly beautiful and pathetically thin, Anne-Marion did something she had always wanted to do: It was the equivalent of a kick. She began telling jokes to make Meridian laugh—because she could not leave her while she looked this way—and when she succeeded, just at the point where Meridian's face lost its magically intriguing gloom, she said, with a very straight face herself, "Meridian, I can not afford to love you. Like the idea of suffering itself, you are obsolete."

Later, though they met again in New York and briefly shared a room, and Meridian had seemed not to remember this parting comment, Anne-Marion continued to think of it as her final word.

After Meridian had gone back South and Anne-Marion discovered herself writing letters to her, making inquiries month after month to find out which town she now lived in and to which address she should send her letters, no one could have been more surprised and confounded than she, who sat down to write each letter as if some heavy object had been attached to her knees, forcing them under her desk, as she wrote with the most galling ferocity, out of guilt and denial and rage.

Truman Held

THE LAST TOAST

I drink to our ruined house,
to the dolor of my life,
to our loneliness together;
and to you I raise my glass,
to lying lips that have betrayed us,
to dead-cold, pitiless eyes,
and to the hard realities:
that the world is brutal and coarse,
that God in fact has not saved us.

—Akhmatova

Truman and Lynne: Time in the South

Lynne: She is sitting on the porch steps of a battered wooden house and black children are all around her. They look, from a distance, like a gigantic flower with revolving human petals. Lynne is the center. Nearer to them Truman notices the children are taking turns combing her hair. Her hair—to them lovely because it is easy to comb—shines, held up behind by black and brown hands as if it is a train. The children might be bridesmaids preparing Lynne for marriage. They do not see him. He frames a picture with his camera but something stops him before he presses the shutter. What stops him he will not, for the moment, have to acknowledge: It is a sinking, hopeless feeling about opposites, and what they do to each other. Suddenly he swings around, and bending on one knee takes a picture of the broken roofing and rusted tin on wood that makes up one wall of a shabby nearby house.

Truman and Lynne: They had a borrowed motorcycle. And on dusky evenings would go zooming down the back roads, the dust powdery and damp on their faces. She wore a helmet, her long hair caught up in back, wisps of it straying across her eyes, slinging itself across her mouth. She held him around the waist and felt his ribs strain against the wind. Through the puffy jacket his body felt fat and thin at the same time. Riding the motorcycle was dangerous because of the whiteness of her face, but at dusk they passed in a blur. At night they were more clear.

To Lynne, the black people of the South were Art. This she begged forgiveness for and tried to hide, but it was no use. To her eyes, used to Northern suburbs where every house looked sterile and identical even before it was completely built, where even the flowers were uniform and their nicknames were already in dictionaries, the shrubs incapable of strong odor or surprise of shape, and the people usually stamped with the seals of their professions; to her, nestled in a big chair made of white oak strips, under a quilt called The Turkey Walk, from Attapulsa, Georgia, in a little wooden Mississippi sharecropper bungalow that had never known paint, the South—and the black people living there—was Art. The songs, the dances, the food, the speech. Oh! She was such a romantic, so in love with the air she breathed, the honeysuckle that grew just beyond the door.

"I will pay for this," she often warned herself. "It is probably a sin to think of a people as Art." And yet, she would stand perfectly still and the sight of a fat black woman singing to herself in a tattered yellow dress, her voice rich and full of yearning, was always—God forgive her, black folks forgive her—the same weepy miracle that Art always was for her.

Truman had had enough of the Movement and the South. But not Lynne. Mississippi—after the disappearance of the three Civil Rights workers in 1964—began to beckon her. For two years she thought of nothing else: If Mississippi is the worst place in America for black people, it stood to reason, she thought, that the Art that was their lives would flourish best there. Truman, who had given up his earlier ambition to live permanently in France, wryly considered Mississippi a just alternative. And so a little over two years after the bodies—battered beyond recognition, except for the colors: two white, one black—of Cheney, Goodman and Schwerner were found hidden in a backwoods Neshoba County, Mississippi, dam, Lynne and Truman arrived.

Of Bitches and Wives

His feelings for Lynne had been undergoing subtle changes for some time. Yet it was not until the shooting of Tommy Odds in Mississippi that he noticed these changes. The shooting of Tommy Odds happened one evening just as he Truman, Tommy Odds and Trilling (a worker from Oklahoma since fled and never seen again) were coming out of the door of the Liberal Trinity Baptist Church. There had been the usual meeting with songs, prayers and strategy for the next day's picketing of downtown stores. They had assumed, also, that guards had been posted; not verifying was their mistake. As they stepped from the church and into the light from an overhanging bulb on the porch, a burst of machine-gun fire came from some bushes across the street. He and Trilling jumped off the sides of the steps. Tommy Odds, in the middle, was shot through the elbow.

When he went to visit Tommy Odds in the hospital he thought, as the elevator carried him to the fourth floor, of how funny it would be when the two of them talked about the frantic jump he and

Trilling made. "You know one thing," he was going to say, laughing, to Tommy Odds, "you're just one *slow* nigger." Then they would wipe the tears of laughter from their eyes and open the bottle of Ripple he had brought. But it had not gone that way at all. First of all, Tommy Odds was not resting up after a flesh wound, as earlier reports had said; he had lost the lower half of his arm. He was propped up in bed now with a clear fluid dripping from a bottle into his other arm. But his horrible gray coloring, his cracked bloodless lips, his glazed eyes, were nothing compared to the utter lack of humor apparent in his face. Impossible to joke, to laugh, without tearing his insides to shreds.

Yet Truman had tried. "Hey, man!" he said, striding across the room with his bottle of Ripple under his arm. "Look what I brought you!" But Tommy Odds did not move his head or his eyes to follow him across the room. He lay looking at a spot slightly above the television, which was high in one corner of the room.

"Lynne says hurry up and get your ass out of here," he continued. "When you get out of here we gon' party for days."

"Don't mention that bitch to me, man," Tommy Odds said.

"What you say?"

"I said"—Tommy Odds turned his head and looked at him, moving his lips carefully so there would be no mistake—"don't mention that bitch to me. Don't mention that white bitch."

"Wait a minute, man," Truman stammered in

surprise, "Lynne had nothing to do with this." And yet, while he was saying this, his tongue was slowed down by thoughts that began twisting like snakes through his brain. How could he say Lynne had nothing to do with the shooting of Tommy Odds, when there were so many levels at which she could be blamed?

"All white people are motherfuckers," said Tommy Odds, as listlessly but clearly as before. "I want to see them destroyed. I could watch their babies being torn limb from limb and I wouldn't lift a finger. The Bible says to dash out the brains of your enemy's children on the rocks. I understand that shit, now."

At this level, Truman thought, sinking into a chair beside his friend, is Lynne guilty? That she is white is true. That she is therefore a killer, evil, a motherfucker—how true? Not true at all! And yet—

"Man, all I do is think about what these crackers did with my motherfucking arm," said Tommy Odds.

"You want me to find out?"

"No, I guess not."

By being white Lynne was guilty of whiteness. He could not reduce the logic any further, in that direction. Then the question was, is it possible to be guilty of a color? Of course black people for years were "guilty" of being black. Slavery was punishment for their "crime." But even if he abandoned this search for Lynne's guilt, because it ended, logically enough, in racism, he was forced to search through other levels for it. For bad or worse, and regardless of what this said about himself as a person, he could not—after his friend's words—keep from thinking Lynne was, in fact, guilty. The thing was to find out how.

"I'm sorry, man," said Tommy Odds. "I shouldn't have come down on your old lady that way."

"It's okay, man, no sweat," Truman mumbled, while his thoughts continued to swirl up, hot and desperate. It was as if Tommy Odds had spoken the words that fit thoughts he had been too cowardly to entertain. On what other level might Lynne, his wife, be guilty?

"It's just that, you know, white folks are a bitch. If I didn't hate them on principle before, I hate them now for personal and concrete reasons. I've been thinking and thinking, lying here. And what I've thought is: Don't nobody offer me marching and preaching as a substitute for going after those jokers' *balls.*"

Was it because she was a white woman that Lynne was guilty? Ah, yes. That was it. Of course. And Truman remembered one night when he and Tommy Odds and Trilling and Lynne had gone to the Moonflower café for a sandwich. They shouldn't have done it, of course. They had been warned against it. They knew better. But there are times in a person's life when to risk everything is the only *affirmation* of life. That night was such a time. What had they been celebrating? Oh, yes. Tommy Odds's niggers-on-the-corner.

For months Tommy Odds had hung out every

Saturday evening at the pool hall on Carver Street, talking and shooting pool. He had been playing with the niggers-on-the-corner for almost a month before he ever opened his mouth about the liberating effects of voting. At first he had been hooted down with shouts of "Man, I don't wanna hear that shit!" and "Man, let's keep this a clean game!" But the good thing about Tommy Odds was his patience. At first he just shut up and worked out with his cue. But in a few days, he'd bring it up again. By the end of the first month his niggers-on-the-corner liked him too much not to listen to him. At the end of three months they'd formed a brigade called "The Niggers-on-the-Corner-Voter-Machine." It was through them that all the derelicts, old grandmamas and grandpas and tough young hustlers and studs, the prostitutes and even the boozy old guy who ran the pool hall registered to vote in the next election. And on this particular Saturday night they decided to celebrate at the Moonflower, a greasy hole-in-the-wall that still had "Whites Only" on its door.

The food was so bad they had not been able to eat it. But they left in high spirits, Lynne giggling about the waitress's hair that was like a helmet made of blonde foil. But as they walked down the street a car slowly followed them until, turning down Carver Street, they were met by some of Tommy Odds's NOTC, who walked them to safety in front of the pool hall. After that night he and Lynne were careful not to be seen together. But since Lynne was the only white woman in town regularly seen only with black people, she was easily identified. He had not thought they would be, too.

So for that night, perhaps Lynne was guilty. But why had she been with them? Had she invited herself? No. Tommy Odds had invited them both to his little party. Even so, it was Lynne's presence that had caused the car to follow them. So she *was* guilty. Guilty of whiteness, as well as stupidity for having agreed to come.

Yet, Lynne loved Tommy Odds, she admired his NOTC. It was Lynne who designed and sewed together those silly badges that they wore, that gave them so much pride.

"What do NOTC mean?" asked the old grandmamas who were escorted like queens down the street to the courthouse.

"Oh, it mean 'Not Only True, but Colored,' " the hustlers replied smoothly. Or, "Not on Time, but Current," said the prostitutes to the old grandpas, letting the old men dig on their cleavage. Or, "Notice of Trinity, with Chirst," the pool sharks said to the religious fanatics, who frowned, otherwise, on pool sharks.

So Lynne was guilty on at least two counts; of being with them, and of being, period. At least that was how Tommy Odds saw it. And who was he to argue, guilty as he was of loving the white bitch who caused his friend to lose his arm?

Thinking this, he shot up from his chair by the bed as if from an electric shock. The bottle of Ripple slipped from his fingers and crashed to the floor.

"Just don't tell me you done wasted the wine,"

said Tommy Odds, groaning. "I was just working myself up for a taste."

"I'll bring another bottle," Truman said, getting towels from the bathroom and mopping up. He cut his finger on a piece of glass and realized he was trembling. When he'd put the waste-wasket outside the door for the janitor he looked back at Tommy Odds. Some small resemblance of his friend remained on the bed. But he could feel the distance that already separated them. When he went out that door they would both be different. He could read the message that Tommy Odds would not, as his former friend, put into words. "Get rid of your bitch, man." That was all.

Getting rid of a bitch is simple, for bitches are dispensable. But getting rid of a wife?

He had read in a magazine just the day before that Lamumba Katurim had gotten rid of his. She was his wife, true, but apparently she was even in that disguise perceived as evil, a castoff. And people admired Lamumba for his perception. It proved his love of his own people, they said. But he was not sure. Perhaps it proved only that Lamumba was fickle. That he'd married his bitch in the first place for shallow reasons. Perhaps he was considering marrying a black woman (as the article said he was) for reasons just as shallow. For how could he state so assuredly that he would marry a black woman next when he did not appear to have any *specific* black woman in mind?

If his own sister told him of her upcoming marriage to Lamumba he would have to know some answers before the nuptial celebration. Like, how many times would Lamumba require her to appear on television with him, or how many times would he parade her before his friends as proof of his blackness.

He thought of Randolph Kay, the Movie Star, who also shucked his white bitch wife, to black applause. But now Randolph Kay *and* his shiny new black wife had moved into the white world completely, to the extent of endorsing the American bombing of civilian targets in Vietnam. Randolph Kay, in fact, now sang love songs to the President! But perhaps it was perverse of him to be so suspicious. Perhaps, after all, he was just trying to cover up his own inability to act as decisively and to the public order as these men had done. No doubt these *were* great men, who perceived, as he could not, that to love the wrong person is an error. If only he could believe it *possible* to love the wrong person he would be home free. As it was, how difficult hating his wife was going to be. He would not even try.

But of course he had.

There was a man he despised, whose name was Tom Johnson. Tom had lived with a white woman for years, only most people didn't know about it. He shuttled her back and forth from his house to a friend's house down the street. Whenever he had important guests, Margaret was nowhere to be found. She was waiting at their friend's house. She was a fleshy blonde, with big tits and a hearty laugh. Once he asked Tom—who was thinking of running for political office—why he didn't marry her. Tom laughed and said, "Boy, you don't understand anything yet. Margaret is a sweet ol' thing. We been living together in harmony for five years. But she's white. Or hadn't you noticed?" Tom had reached out a chubby hand to bring Truman's head closer to his own and his small eyes danced. "It's just a matter of pussy. That's all. Just a matter of my *personal* taste in pussy." And then he had pulled Truman's head even closer and said with conspiratorial glee," It's *good* stuff. Want some?"

"I used to believe that—" he had begun, but Tom cut him off.

"This is war, man, *war!* And all's fair that fucks with the suckers' minds!"

Then he had begun to see them together. Not in public, but with small groups of men, in the back rooms of bars. Margaret could play poker and he liked to see her when she won. She jumped up, squealing, in her small-girl voice, her big tits bouncing at the top of her low-cut blouse, and all the men looked at her tolerantly, in amusement, their curiosity about her big body already at rest. After what Tom had told him this did not surprise him: the exhibition of her delight in winning, the men's amused solidarity, their willingness to share her in this position of secrecy. And Margaret? Those squeals of delight—what did she feel? Or was it unmanly, unblack now, even to care, to ask?

When the community center was built, he began painting a mural of the struggle along one wall. The young men who would use the center for dances, Ping-Pong, card games, etc., were building tables and chairs. They were a shy, sweet bunch, country boys and naive as possible, who were literally afraid of white women. Their first meeting with Lynne had been comic. Nobody wanted to be seen talking to her alone, and even as a group they would only talk to her from a distance. She could, just by speaking to them and walking up to them as she spoke, force them back twenty yards. This shamed him now, as he thought of Tommy Odds.

Why should they be afraid of her? She was just a woman. Only they could not see her that way. To them she was a route to Death, pure and simple. They felt her power over them in their bones; their mothers had feared her even before they were born. Watching their fear of her, though, he saw a strange thing: They did not even see her as a human being, but as some kind of large, mysterious doll. A thing of movies and television, of billboards and car and soap commercials. They liked her hair, not because it was especially pretty, but because it was long. To them, *length* was beauty. They loved the tails of horses.

Against this fear, Lynne used her considerable charm. She baked cookies for them, allowed them to drink wine in her house, and played basketball with them at the center. Jumping about in her shorts, tossing her long hair, she laughed and sweated and shouted and cursed. She forced them to like her.

But while this building of trust and mutual liking was coming into being, the Movement itself was changing. Lynne was no longer welcome at any of the meetings. She was excluded from the marches. She was no longer allowed to write articles for the paper. She spent most of her time in the center or at home. The boys, unsure now what their position as young black men should be, remained inexplicably loyal. They came to visit her, bringing news she otherwise would not have heard. For Truman too was under pressure of ostracism from the group, and though he remained a member of all Movement discussions it was understood he would say nothing to his wife.

The New York Times

He had gone to Meridian three years after he married Lynne, driving across from Mississippi to a small town in Alabama where Meridian, at that time, lived. She had still owned a few possessions then, and was teaching in a Freedom school and keeping rather than burning her poems. He had begged her, or tried to beg her (because she did not seem to understand what begging constituted), to give him another chance. She loved him, he rashly assumed—as she smiled at him—and he did not see why she should deny herself.

"For Lynne's sake alone, I couldn't do it," she had said languidly, rocking slowly in her yellow chair. "What does she have now besides you?"

"Everything," he said sarcastically. "She's still an American white woman."

"Is that so easy?" asked Meridian, stopping her rocking, turning away from him toward the window. The light exposed small petal-shaped flecks of black in her brown eyes. "She was that when she decided she'd rather have you than everything. True? Or not?"

"How can you take her side?"

"Her side? I'm sure she's already taken it. I'm trying to make the acquaintance of my side in all this. What side *is* mine?" She was not uptight. Nothing trembled. She thought. Rocked. "Don't you think you owe something to Camara?" She looked him square in the eye.

"I owe more to all the little black kids being blown away by whitey's racism."

"Of which your daughter is one, surely?" She steadied the rocker, listened.

"Besides," he continued, "I don't love Lynne the way I do you. You notice I don't lie and say I don't love her *at all.* She's meant a great deal to me. But you're different. *Loving* you is different—"

"Because I'm black?"

"You make me feel healthy, purposeful—"

"Because I'm black?"

"Because you're *you,* damn it! The woman I should have married and didn't!"

"Should have *loved,* and didn't," she murmured.

And Truman sank back staring, as if at a lifeboat receding in the distance.

Truman had felt hemmed in and pressed down by Lynne's intelligence. Her inability to curb herself, her imagination, her wishes and dreams. It came to her, this lack of restraint, which he so admired at first and had been so refreshed by, because she had never been refused the exercise of it. She assumed that nothing she could discover was capable of destroying her. He was charmed by her presumption; still, he was not prepared to love her over a long period, but for a short one.

How marvelous it was at first to find that she read everything. That she thought, deeply. That she longed to put her body on the line for his freedom. How her idealism had warmed him, brought him into the world, made him eager to tuck her under his wing, under himself, sheltering her from her own illusions. Her awareness of wrong, her indignant political response to whatever caused him to suffer, was a definite part of her charm, and yet he preferred it as a part of her rarely glimpsed, commented upon in passing, as one might speak of the fact that Lenin wore a beard. And as she annoyed him with her irrepressible questions that kept bursting out and bubbling up into their lives, like spring water rising beside a reservoir and undermining the concrete of the dam, he had thought of Meridian, whom he imagined as more calm, predictable. Her shy, thin grace, her relative inarticulateness (Lynne, by comparison, never seemed to stop talking, and her accent was unpleasant), her brown strength that he imagined would not mind being a resource for someone else. . . . In Meridian, all the things lacking in Lynne seemed apparent. Here was a woman to rest in, as a ship must have a port. As a train must have a shed.

He was stunned to learn that she had long ago dismissed him. In fact, when he looked into her eyes, he knew he was remembering someone else, someone he had made up. Why, he had not known this woman at all! For the first time he detected a quality in Meridian that Lynne—who had known her only briefly—had insisted anyone could see. Meridian, no matter what she was saying to you, and no matter what you were saying to her, seemed to be thinking of something else, another conversation perhaps, an earlier one, that continued on a parallel track. Or of a future one that was running an identical course. This was always true.

There was also something dark, Truman thought, a shadow, that seemed to swing, like the pendulum of a clock, or like a blade, behind her open, candid eyes, that made one feel condemned. That made one think of the guillotine. That made one suspect she was unbalanced. When he noticed it he felt a shrinking, a retreating of his balls: He wanted her still, but would not have wanted (or been able) to make love to her.

And in front of this restlessness behind her eyes, this obvious mental activity, she placed a deceptive outer calm. He knew that in this woman who never seemed to hurry, and whom he was destined to pursue, the future might be short, but memory was very long.

He groaned. Mightily, and at length.

"Oh no," Meridian said pleasantly. "You wanted a virgin, don't you remember?" (He could remember nothing of the kind.) "You wanted a woman who was not 'sexually promiscuous.' " (When had he said he wanted that?) "But on the other hand, you wanted a woman who had had worldly experiences . . . to match your own. Now, since I already had a son, whose existence you frightened me into denying, and since you also wanted to make love to me, and since I had no worldly experience to speak of, marriage between us never reached the point of discussion. In Lynne you captured your ideal: a virgin who was eager for sex and well-to-do enough to have had 'worldly experiences.' " She explained this in the voice of instruction.

What she said was absolutely true. Though he was positive he had never told her any of these things. He *had* wanted a virgin, had been raised to expect and *demand* a virgin; and never once had he questioned this. He had been as predatory as the other young men he ran with, as eager to seduce and devirginize as they. Where had he expected his virgin to come from? Heaven?

When he made love to Meridian it had been almost impossible to penetrate her; it was as if her vagina were sealed shut by a taut muscle that fought him. Afterward there was no blood and although she had not said she was a virgin, he had assumed it. It was only later that he could begin to understand why her vagina had been clenched so tightly against him. She had been spasmodic with fear. Fear because sex was always fraught with ugly consequences for her, and fear because if she did not make love with him she might lose him, and if she did make love with him he might lose interest. As he must have seemed, to her, to have done.

But the truth was different. After they had made love, he learned she had been married and had had a child. How could he have a wife who already had a child? And that she had given that child away.

What repugnance there arose in him for her. For her eyes which, he thought, burned unnaturally bright. For her thin body on which her breasts (which he much admired) hung much too heavily: When he knew about the child he thought of her breasts as used jugs. They had belonged to some other man.

He had wanted a woman perfect in all the eyes of the world, not a savage who bore her offspring and hid it. *And yet,* had she approached him on the street, dragging her child with her by the hand, he would never have glanced at her. For him she would not even have existed as a woman he might love.

Ironically, it was this awareness of his own limitation, which grew keener year by year, that caused Meridian to remain, a constant reproach, in his thoughts. Wherever he was he would think of her face, her body, the way her hands had fluttered over his back when she kissed him. He thought of the times she had seemed embarrassed for him and he did not know why. He thought of how frequently he had felt superior to her. There was one memory in particular that pained him: Years ago when he was dating the white exchange students she had asked him, the words blurted out in so thick a shame he knew she intended to forget she'd ever asked—"But what do you *see* in them?"

And he had replied cruelly, thoughtlessly, in a way designed to make her despise the confines of her own provincial mind:

"They read *The New York Times.*"

Truman felt that that exchange, too, rested somewhere behind Meridian's eyes. It would have been joy to him to forget her, as it would have been joy never to have been his former self. But running away from Lynne, at every opportunity, and existing a few days in Meridian's presence, was the best that he could do.

Visits

The summer before Meridian arrived in Chicokema, which was near the Georgia coast, Lynne visited her. They had not seen each other since the death of Lynne and Truman's daughter, Camara, a year earlier. Meridian was living in an adequately furnished house that the black community—having witnessed one of her performances and the paralysis that followed it—provided. The house was in an obscure farming village on the Georgia-Alabama line, and how Lynne tracked her there Meridian was at first unable to imagine. The simple answer was that Truman, who was also visiting her at that time, and whose visits had become so commonplace she hardly noticed them, had apparently phoned her.

There were periods in Meridian's life when it could not be perceived that she was ill. It was true that she'd lost so much of her hair that finally she had shaved her head and begun wearing a striped white and black railroad worker's cap: the cotton was durable and light and the visor shaded her eyes from the sun. And it was also true that she was frail and sickly-looking. But among the impoverished, badly nourished black villagers—who attempted to thrive on a diet of salt meat and potatoes during the winter, and fresh vegetables without meat during the summer—she did not look out of place. In fact, she looked as if she belonged.

Like them, she could summon whatever energy a task that had to be performed required, and like them, this ability seemed to her something her ancestors had passed on from the days of slavery when there had been no such thing as a sick slave, only a "malingering" one. Like the luckless small farmers around her who tended their crops "around the weather"—sitting out the days of rain, rushing out to plant or chop or harvest when the sun came out—she lived "around" her illness. Like them, it seemed pointless to her to complain.

Meridian wondered who the stout white woman could be, knocking at her door as if her fist were made of iron. Then she saw that it was Lynne, a great deal changed.

"I'll make us some tea," she said, inviting her in.

"Thanks, Meridian," said Lynne, unburdening herself of her satchel bag and flopping heavily onto the couch. "I'm exhausted!"

She wore a long Indian bedspread skirt—yellow, with brown and black elephants—and a loose black blouse embroidered with flowers and small mirrors around the neck. Intricately worked gold earrings dangled against her neck. Her olive complexion, which tanned golden in a day of sun, was now chalk-white, her eyes were red-veined and her eyelids drooped. Her dark hair was tangled and dull.

"I haven't slept for three motherfuckin' *days,*" said Lynne.

"You should have stopped at one of those new Scottish Inns. They're cheap."

"Not cheap if you're broke," Lynne said flatly, looking about the room, her eyes resting for a moment on one of Meridian's broadside poems which she had stapled to the wall. It was the last object of personal value Meridian owned, and she intended, when she vacated the house, to leave it there.

"Truman's here, you know," Meridian said, bringing in the tea. She had added bologna and light bread, the two foods people donated to her upkeep wherever she went, and a peanut butter and jelly sandwich. Lynne began eating the bologna without the bread, which was white and spongy, rolled up like a wiener. Then she licked the jelly from the peanut butter, poking at it delicately but never missing, like a cat.

"I thought he might be," she said, all attention focused on her food.

"Really, Lynne, there's not the slightest thing between us. We're as innocent as brother and sister." Meridian stopped. Perhaps that was not as innocent as it might sound. "There's nothing between us."

"I know there's nothing between you." Lynne laughed, a short bark that ended in a cough. Her voice was hoarse from smoking and her top lip curled back in a way Meridian did not remember.

"That's why he flies to you like a goddamn homing pigeon. Nothing between you, my ass." She had almost said "but my ass."

"Lynne . . ."

"There'll *always* be something between you." Lynne laughed again, and pulled out a cigarette. "Maybe you *don't* know what it is," she said with some surprise, but with more undisguised cynicism. "What's between you is everything that could have happened and didn't, because you were both scared to death of each other. Black men and women *are* scared to death of each other, you know. Not your *average* black men and women, of course, who accept each other as only natural, but people like you and Truman who have to keep analyzing each other's problems. People like you and Truman ought to lock yourselves up in a room somewhere and smoke yourselves silly, fall into each other's black arms and fuck your brains out." She frowned. "Of course, you all do have that super-long line of failure in y'all's personal relationships. That must be hard to go against. Or maybe it's just too many blonde white women selling foot powder and Noxzema shaving cream. Did you know that Truman prefers blondes? I think he does. . . ." She inhaled deeply and slowly let out the smoke.

"It must be deep," she said after a pause. "He married me, and keeps trying to screw himself to death all over the place, and you—well, who knows what you do with yourself. . . . I don't blame you though, for not getting married. That was real smart. *Real* smart. I wish somebody'd let me turn in my oaths. It was a shitty arrangement, after we had the kid." She lifted her teacup and put it down without tasting.

"I've gained weight, haven't I?" she asked.

"We've all gained," said Meridian, "or lost."

"Well, you sure haven't gained," said Lynne, glancing sharply at her, "in fact, you—"

"You just can't see it," said Meridian, deliberately cutting her off. She knew what she looked like; it didn't bother her; but she did not wish to hear Lynne comment on it.

"And my hair is turning gray," said Lynne. "I have gray strands all across the top. I started to dye it once. You know, it is so hard to live with myself, looking old so quick." She reached up to touch the almost invisible strands of gray at her temples.

"You've had a hard life," said Meridian.

"The only people who ever loved me," Lynne continued absently, looking about for a mirror, "were the po' folks down in the woods, the swamps. They never looked down on me. Never despised me. After I had Camara I brought her back down here one time to show her off and they loved us both. Didn't despise us. Didn't try to make us feel we had stolen one of y'all's scarce few men. Made us feel like family. Of course they were the old type of black people, like that old religious lady who fed us that time. Remember her? They just came out on the porch and said: 'Y'all *come* in. Here, girl, let me *see* this big old fine baby. What you name her? Ca*ma*ra. Now that's *real* cute. Lord, ain't she got a head of *hair.* And will you *look* at them big eyes. Just as *brown.* Naw, I think they's *green.* Naw, I believe they *is* brown. Well, just come on to your kinfolk. Come on here. That's right.' "

Lynne was beginning to weep. Tears slid off her chin.

"It looks more like it was bleached in the sun," said Meridian.

"Never made us feel like there was nobody on earth so low as to want us. Me and my brown sugar baby. 'Hair,' she said, coming back, 'looks like it was bleached in the sun'—my ass. Kind, polite, courteous—that's that Southern charm folks down here have. It's such shit."

"Truman is out with his camera. He really should be back any minute."

"With his camera! Probably taking pictures of all the poor little girls he'd like to fuck. That's his only interest in the poor. Not to mention the black." She wiped her eyes and lifted her cup in a salute.

"I forgot sugar," said Meridian, rising and going into the kitchen.

"Mustn't forget *sugar,*" said Lynne. "*Oy vey,* you're a regular Betty Crocker. How do y'all do it, I wonder? Always gracious and calm. Perfect little ladies; whether you lived in the big house as Big Missy or as slave. It must've been all that corn bread. Made y'all mealy-mouthed."

"I didn't invite Truman," said Meridian. "I never have."

"I don't care about Truman," said Lynne, lighting up a reefer and taking a deep drag. "I don't care about the son of a bitch any more."

Meridian watched them meet in her back yard. They did not smile or touch. Truman was frowning, Lynne's face was tense. Meridian stood in the center of the living room and began doing exercises. First she pretended she was slowly jumping rope, bouncing lightly off the floor and springing into the air. Then she touched her toes. Then she lay down and began raising first one leg and then the other, holding them suspended to the count of ten.

"What the fuck do you mean, nigger?" Lynne's voice, harsh and wild, came from the back yard. It dropped into the quietness of the neighborhood like a stone.

"Will you shut the fuck up, *beast.*"

"Not until you tell me why I can't ever find you unless I look in Meridian's back yard."

"I don't live with you. I don't have to explain myself to you. Not any more, I don't."

"Look at me!" she said, foolishly, since he *was* looking at her. "You think you can step over me and just keep going . . . ruin my life."

"Don't bring up your lousy dancing career," he snarled. "If you people could dance you wouldn't have to copy us all the time."

"You asshole," she said. "You're a fine one to talk. You're the only nigger in the Free World who can't dance a lick. Every time you get out there shaking your ass you look like a faggot with cramps."

His voice was suddenly menacing: "Cut out the 'nigger' shit."

"I could have made it," she said. "At least I could have stayed healthy."

"You always needed a shrink," he said. "It's symptomatic of your race."

Lynne had begun to cry, wiping her nose on the edge of her skirt. Truman watched with disgust.

"My race? My *race?*" Lynne turned her face up as if imploring the trees. She laughed in spite of herself.

He had never hated, aesthetically, the whiteness of Lynne so much. It shocked him. Her nose was red and peeling, her hair was stringy and—he scrutinized it quickly—there was some gray! And she was so stout! Stouter even than the last time he'd seen her, after Camara died. He could not stop himself from thinking she looked very much like a pig. Her eyes seemed tinier than he'd ever seen them and her white ears needed only to grow longer and flop over a bit.

But what was happening (had happened) to him, that he should have these thoughts? There was a large pecan tree beside him. He leaned against it.

"Lynne," he said finally, "why don't you go on back home? There's nothing between me and Meridian. Not like you think. She doesn't understand why I keep bothering her any more than I do."

"Bull."

"Meridian is my past, my *sister* . . ." Truman began, but Lynne cut him off.

"I've heard all that shit before," she said. "But it doesn't speak to what you did to me and Camara. Running off as soon as black became beautiful . . ."

It was his turn to laugh. "You don't *believe* that?" he asked.

"You bet your stinking life I do. You must think I'm stupid. You only married me because you were too much of a coward to throw a bomb at all the crackers who make you sick. You're like the rest of those nigger zombies. No life of your own at all unless it's something against white folks. You can't even enjoy a good fuck without hoping some cracker is somewhere grinding his teeth."

"I married you because I loved you."

"Yeah, and you wanted something *strange* around the house to entertain your friends."

"Shut up, Lynne," said Truman, as he saw Meridian coming out of the house.

"I'm going for a walk," said Meridian to Lynne. "But if you're sleepy or tired you can take a nap on the couch in the living room. I'll leave the door open."

"Doesn't True look well?" Lynne asked, as Meridian stood watching them. She had not been able to ignore their loud voices and was annoyed with them.

"He looks divine," she said.

"So *mature,*" said Lynne, "yet so young . . . don't you think? You're thirty-four now, aren't you, darlin'?" she asked, turning briefly to Truman, who scowled at her. "Would you believe he's heading for middle age? I wouldn't. It comes from easy living and of course he's a vampire. Sucks the blood of young white virgins to keep him vigorous. Did you know that?" She turned a bright, tight face to Truman. "Tell her about this thing you have, darlin' (and of course he's not the only one), for young white virgins. And don't lie and say I wasn't one."

"Shut *up*!"

"You Southern girls lead such sheltered lives," Lynne said, affecting a Southern belle accent and twirling a lock of her unwashed, rather oily hair around her finger, "I declare I'd be just bored to death. That's why your men come North, sugah, looking for that young white meat that proves they have arrived. You know? Tell me, how does it feel to be a complete *flop*" (this said with a Bette Davis turn of her wrist) "at keeping your men?

"You know, I could—yes, fat ass 'n' all, walk up the street anywhere around here and Hey Presto! I'd have all y'all's men following after me, their little black tongues hanging out."

Truman felt as if his soul, hanging precariously for a lifetime, had fallen off the shelf.

"It would take a sick mind to be pleased with that old racist chestnut, you silly heifer." He would have liked the power to wither her, literally, with a glance.

Lynne took out her sunglasses and put them on, smiling and nodding, as if her audience were large.

"Bra*vo*!" she said. "Underneath that old-fashioned cullud exterior beats the heart of a murderer. I knew it."

"Forgive me, both of you," said Meridian, "but I'm locking the house."

"A locked house, a locked pussy," said Lynne, giggling.

"I didn't mean anything by it, Meridian," said Lynne, later, crying into the pillows of the couch. "It's just that you have everything. I mean, you're so strong, your people love you, and you can cope. I don't have anything. I gave up everything for True, and he just shit on me."

She had stayed in the yard arguing with Truman until he walked away. Then she had gotten into Meridian's house through an open window. Just like these country bumpkins, she thought, to lock the door and leave the window wide open.

Meridian had walked until she wore herself out, and one thought had preoccupied her mind: "The only new thing now," she had said to herself, mumbling it aloud, so that people turned to stare at her, "would be the refusal of Christ to accept crucifixion. King," she had said, turning down a muddy lane, "should have refused. Malcolm, too, should have refused. All those characters in all those novels that require death to end the book should refuse. All saints should walk away. Do their bit, then—just walk away. See Europe, visit Hawaii, become agronomists or raise Dalmatians." She didn't care what they did, but they should do it.

She looked at Lynne, who was definitely not yet a saint. She did not know what Lynne should do. She was too tired, at the moment, to care.

"Listen," said Lynne, "when Camara and I lived in the East Village—oh hell, Lower East Side, on 12th Street—I couldn't walk down the street to take her to kindergarten without niggers wanting to jump me. What could I do? I'm a woman, right?

They never let up until they got me in bed. Then the crying and the pleading when I didn't feel like giving'em any. So usually I just said Fuck it! I've got to get some sleep. So get on up on me, nigger. Just don't take all night. Sometimes I'd go to sleep with'em still at it."

"*Must* you say nigger?" Meridian asked wearily. She realized that among many hip people the use of the word was not considered offensive but rather a matter of style. That she would hate it till the dirt was thrown over her face she knew mattered not at all to people who would eventually appropriate anything they could laugh at, or talk about, or wear. "Why did you let these people in, if you didn't want to be bothered?"

"Aw, I don't know. I got so tired. Begging, listening to people begging, is tiring. Besides, you don't know what's going on in the cities. There are all these white girls that are so fucked up with guilt they're willing and happy to keep a black guy, even if he's obviously a junkie bum. Not like me, at least I try for the classier bums—like the old poets and jazz stars of yesteryear. Like—"

"Don't give me any names," said Meridian. "Believe me when I say I don't want to know."

"I don't freak myself out, analyzing everything I do. What's a screw between friends, anyhow?"

"Between friends would be different."

"You can't understand. Your life is so . . . there's something wrong with your life, you know. It's so, so, pro*scribed.* Like you drew a circle around it and only walk as far as the edge. Why did you come back down here? What are you looking for? These people will always be the same. You can't change them. Nothing will."

"But I can change," said Meridian. "I hope I will."

"I live for the moment, no looking back for me. Take what life offers . . . ah shit! It's just that my life is so fucked up. Truman was the only stable thing in it. I don't even have a photograph of my folks." Lynne's eyes narrowed. "Not that I need one to remember them. All I have to do is close my eyes and I see them all too well.

"My father was, actually, my father was wonderful—at least I thought he was wonderful. He wasn't your dashing prince, but in his dull, careful, Jewish way, he was terrific. He never spoke more than a dozen words to me in anger, all the time I was growing up. Always so gentle, so fair. I couldn't believe it when I called to tell them Camara had been attacked and died. You know what he said? My mother wouldn't even speak to me, although she could tell I was crying. My father took the phone and asked me to repeat. I told him my daughter was dead and he said, 'So's our daughter,' meaning me! And when I stopped breathing, because I thought I'd heard wrong, he said—as calmly as anything—'*Nu?* So what else?' " Lynne was eating grapes, she spat out a grape seed. "The heartless bastard, the least he could have done was prepare me for the creep he turned out to be. Fathers suck," she added, frowning. "When my old Tata is dead, then I'll remember his kindness. I refuse to do so until then.

"Mothers are beasts, too," continued Lynne. "All my mother thinks about is herself as perceived by the neighbors."

Meridian sat deep in her chair, her legs had fallen asleep. "It's all behind you," she said.

"You don't know the half," said Lynne, darting a glance at her. "Really you don't."

Sleepy, puzzled, off-guard, Meridian stared at her.

"Truman said one of my fantasies was being raped by a black man. That was what he reduced everything to. But it *wasn't!*" Her eyes, pleading, were filled with tears. She sat up on the couch and wiped her eyes. "You're the only one I can talk to about it. The only one who would believe it wasn't my fault that it happened. True let one of his friends . . ."

"I can't listen to this," said Meridian, rising abruptly and throwing up her hands. "I'm sorry, I just can't."

"Wait a minute," cried Lynne. "I know you're thinking about lynchings and the way white women have always lied about black men raping them. Maybe this wasn't rape. I don't know. I think it was. It *felt* like it was."

Meridian sat down again and looked at Lynne through her fingers, which were spread, like claws, over her face.

"Can't you understand I can't listen to you? Can't you understand there are some things I don't want to know?"

"You wouldn't believe me *either*?" Lynne asked.

"No," Meridian said, coldly.

"Well fuck you."

"Go to bed, Lynne. Why don't you go to bed?"

But Lynne did not intend to leave the room. Perhaps Meridian wouldn't listen to her, but she could sit there herself and try to remember what had happened to her and Truman's life.

Lynne

She remembered it was spring, and she had left her parents' house, she hoped, for good. And if this hope was not to become reality she did not intend to struggle over it or care. They headed south over the Interstate, their old car, a venerable black ruin, loaded down with her books, his paints, rolls of canvas, two cameras, and filled with music from a black radio station in Newark that, miraculously, they held until they reached the vicinity of the Maryland border.

For six months they'd met secretly in his mother's house. His room at the top of the stairs, the paintings—by Romare Bearden, Charles White, Jacob Lawrence—on the walls, as familiar to her as her own room across town. More familiar, because her room seemed still to be the hideout of a sixteen-year-old kid—with dancing shoes, tights, paper flowers from some forgotten high school decoration, and the faces of movie stars her mother encouraged her to like. No black faces, of course (though she had once had a picture of Sammy Davis, Jr., and Mai), which was not unusual. Not even any really Jewish faces, for that matter. No faces as dark, ripening, lean and high-nosed as her own. A *young* room, fresh, tacky, that wore innocence like the wrong shade of face powder, youth beneath the pink canopied bed like a bright rose preserved under glass. And she—entering her room—felt now a superiority to it, as if she now knew more (since her relationship with Truman) than the room was capable of containing. For although it was her room, it was in her mother's house. Vulnerable to search and seizure, and the contemplative scrutiny of her mother's always uneasy mind.

When her mother tracked her to Truman's house they heard her screaming from three blocks away, because it was then that her mother noticed she had tracked her only daughter—who had slipped out of the house as furtively as a rabbi from a pogrom—to a black neighborhood. And she had screamed without ceasing, without, seemingly, even stopping to inhale, all the way to the Helds' steps. Where she had paused long enough to press the bell, the ringing of the bell itself like a blunter bellowing of her anguish. That harsh buzz, followed by the continuation of her mother's, by then, howl, rested in the back of Lynne's brain like a spinning record on which the sound was turned down. It would never leave her, even when she was most happy. Like the birth cry to a lucid mother it existed simultaneously with the growth of herself away from and apart from her mother. When she died she knew it would still be spinning soundlessly there.

Tommy Odds

"Altuna *Jones?*" Tommy Odds laughed. "*Hedge* Phillips, and what was that other guy's name?" He stood over her while she sewed, his usually sad black eyes brightly twinkling.

"I bet them guys never saw nobody like you. And if they did they never would let on. I bet you're scaring them niggers to death in them shorts."

He was only half-playful because he disliked what whites in the Movement chose to wear in black communities. A girl who had volunteered to take notes at church meetings had liked to sit with her dress pulled up so high you could see her drawers. This she did in the amen corner. The pious old women and hacked-down prayerful old men had hardly been able to express their grievances. And she, a blonde with a blank, German face—had placidly chewed gum and scratched her thighs, oblivious to what was hanging the people up. And of course nobody dared tell her. It wasn't fear. They were simply too polite to tell a guest in their community that she was behaving like a tramp.

Tommy Odds looked at Lynne carefully. She had tanned since coming South. She seemed relaxed and happy. He thought of her life with Truman—how they could never ride on the same seat of their car, but must always sit as if one of them were chauffeuring the other. And there was no entertainment for them at night. They were too poor to own a television set. But they seemed content. Truman with his sculpting and building the recreation center. Lynne writing poems occasionally, reading them to her friends, then tearing them up. Sometimes she would paste an especially good one—one she liked—in front of the commode, at eye level. You had no choice but to read it. These were usually love poems to Truman, or poems about the need for gentleness in the heart of the Revolution. Her favorite book was Jane Stembridge's plea for love and community, *I Play Flute*. It was clear also in her poetry and in the things she said that to her black people had a unique beauty, a kind of last-gasp loveliness, which, in other races, had already become extinct.

He had wanted to make love to her. Because she was white, first of all, which meant she would assume she was in control, and because he wanted—at first—to force her to have him in ways that would disgust and thrill her. He thought of hanging her from a tree by her long hair and letting her weight gradually pull the hair from her scalp. He wondered if that would eventually happen to a person hung up in that way.

But Lynne grew on him, as she did on everyone. And she was a good worker. Better—to be honest—

than the black women who always wanted to argue a point instead of doing what they were told. And she liked doing things for him; it was almost as if she knew he must be placated, obeyed. She had sewed the armbands willingly, and listened to his teasing enthusiastically, and tried to be carefree and not too Northern or hip. And she had worn her hair—for some strange reason that amounted almost to a premonition—in tight braids that she pinned securely to the top of her head.

Lynne

For of course it was Tommy Odds who raped her. As he said, it wasn't really rape. She had not screamed once, or even struggled very much. To her, it was worse than rape because she felt circumstances had not permitted her to scream. As Tommy Odds said, he was just a lonely one-arm nigger down on his luck that nobody had time for any more. But she would have time—wouldn't she? Because she was not like those rough black women who refused to be sympathetic and sleep with him—was she? She would be kind and not like those women or any other women who turned him down because they were repulsed and prejudiced and the maroon stump of his arm made them sick. She would be a true woman and save him—wouldn't she?

"But Tommy *Odds*," she pleaded, pushing against his chest, "I'm married to your friend. You can't *do* this."

"You don't have to tell him," he said, undoing her braids and wrapping his hand twice in her hair. "Kiss me," he said, pulling her against him. Water stood in her eyes as she felt her hair being tugged out at the roots.

"Please don't do this," she whimpered softly.

"You *knows* I cain't hep mysef," he said in loose-lipped mockery, looking at her red cheeks where tiny red capillaries ran swollen and broken. His eyes were sly, half-closed, filled with a sensuousness that was ice-cold. "You're so white and red, like a pretty little ol' pig." He lifted her briefly by her hair, pulled her closer to him.

"Tommy Odds—"

"Put your arms around me," he said, "and tell me you love me."

"Tommy Odds *please.*" She was crying aloud now and when she flailed her arms she bumped against his stump. Her throat worked.

"It makes you sick?" asked Tommy Odds. "You think I'm a cripple? Or is it just that you really don't dig niggers? Ones darker than your old man?"

"You know that's not true," she groaned.

He had tripped her back onto the bed and was pulling up her skirt with his teeth. His hand came out of her hair and was quickly inside her blouse. He pinched her nipples until they stung.

"*Please,*" she begged.

"I didn't really mean that," he said. "I know your heart is in the right place" (sucking her left nipple). "You're not like the others."

"God—" she said.

There was a moment when she knew she could force him from her. But it was a flash. She lay instead thinking of his feelings, his hardships, of the way he was black and belonged to people who lived without hope; she thought about the loss of his arm. She felt her own guilt. And he entered her and she did not any longer resist but tried instead to think of Tommy Odds as he was when he was her friend—and near the end her arms stole around his neck, and before he left she told him she forgave him and she kissed his slick rounded stump that was the color of baked liver, and he smiled at her from far away, and she did not know him. "Be seein' you," he said.

The next day Tommy Odds appeared with Raymond, Altuna and Hedge.

"Lynne," he said, pushing the three boys in front of him into the room, "I'm going to show you what you are."

She thought, helplessly, as if it were waiting for just this moment to emerge from her memory, of a racist painting she had once seen in *Esquire* of a nude white woman spread-eagled on a rooftop surrounded by black men. She thought: *gang rape.* Her anal muscles tightened, her throat closed with an audible choking sound.

"What do you want?" she asked, looking—for the first time—downward toward the genitals of Hedge and Altuna and Raymond. They were looking sideways at her, as if embarrassed. All of them had been smoking grass, she smelled it on them.

Pointing to her body as if it were conquered territory, Tommy Odds attempted to interest the boys in exploring it: "Tits," he said, flicking them with his fingers, "ass."

"What do you want?" demanded Lynne, furious because seeing the faces of Altuna, Hedge and Raymond through the front window had reassured her, and she had not locked her door.

"What did we do yesterday afternoon?" Tommy asked lazily, idly, holding the back of her neck. "What did I do?"

Lynne gathered her courage. "You raped me."

"Um hum," he said, smiling at the boys who were attentive, curious and silent, as if holding their breath. "And what did you do when I was getting ready to get out of you?"

She did not reply. He squeezed her neck.

"I—" she began.

"A little nine-year-old black girl was raped by a white animal last week in Tchula," said Tommy Odds, "they pulled her out of the river, dead, with a stick shoved up her. Now that was rape. Not like us." He tightened his grip. "Tell us, bitch, what did you do when it started getting good to you?"

"It was never good," said Lynne. Then, "I kissed your arm."

"My stub," he corrected her. "You hugged me and you kissed my stub. And what else did you do?"

He was holding her neck in the crook of his elbow, her chin was pointed at the ceiling. He squeezed.

"I forgave you," said Lynne.

Tommy Odds laughed. "Forgave *me*," he said.

"Yes," said Lynne.

He loosened his grip. They stood together now, his arm around her shoulders, his fingers lightly stroking her breast. From the reflection in the windowpane they appeared to be a couple. Lynne looked into the horrified faces of Altuna, Hedge and Raymond. But perhaps, she thought, they are not horrified. Perhaps that is not a true reading of what I see on their faces (for the first time it seemed to her that black features were grossly different—more sullen and cruel—than white). Though none of them smiled, she could have sworn they were grinning. She imagined their gleaming teeth, with sharp, pointed edges. Oh, God, she thought, what a racist cliché.

"You want it?" Tommy Odds asked the boys.

Lynne closed her eyes. She could not imagine they would say no. The whole scene flashed before her. She was in the center of the racist *Esquire* painting, her white body offered up as a sacrifice to black despair. She thought of the force, the humiliation, the black power. These boys were no longer her friends; the sight of her naked would turn them into savages.

"Go on," said Tommy Odds. "Have some of it."

Altuna Jones—whose head was shaped exactly like a person's head would be shaped with such a name, like a melon, long, and with close-cut hair—cleared his throat.

"It? *It?*" he said. "What *it* you talking about? That ain't no *it*, that's Lynne."

Hedge Phillips spoke. Like his name there was evasion in his looks. He was short and fat and so oily black his features were hard to distinguish until he smiled. When he talked one foot stroked the ground experimentally, as if eager to move off down the street.

"We not gon' hurt you," he said to Lynne. "Us thought it was a party here this evening."

Raymond, shyer even than the other two, but grasping somehow that a masculine line, no matter how weak, must be taken, said, plaintively as it turned out, to Tommy Odds, "You *know*, Tommy, that I have a girlfriend."

"Look," said Odds, with contempt, "she's nothing particular. You guys are afraid of her, that's all. Shit. Crackers been raping your mamas and sisters for generations and here's your chance to get off on a piece of their goods."

"Man, you crazy," said Altuna Jones, and he looked at Lynne with pity, for she had obviously not been—in his opinion—raped. All his life he had heard it was not possible to rape a woman without killing her. To him, in fact, rape meant that you fucked a corpse. That Lynne would actually stoop to sleeping with Tommy Odds meant something terrible was wrong with her, and he was sorry.

The three boys left.

"They're not like you," said Lynne, though she had barely finished thinking they would be exactly like Tommy Odds. "They don't need to rape white women to prove they're somebody."

"Rape," said Tommy Odds. "I fucked you. *We* fucked."

Again he pressed her down on the bed and fumbled with her clothes. Even before she began to fight him off she knew she would not have to. Tommy Odds was impotent. He spat in her face, urinated on the floor, and left her lying there.

When Truman came home again, Lynne could not talk about it. She could hardly talk at all. She was packed and ready to leave. She wished she could go to the police, but she was more afraid of them than she was of Tommy Odds, because they would attack young black men in the community indiscriminately, and the people she wanted most to see protected would suffer. Besides, she thought as long as she didn't tell, Truman would never know. It would hurt him, she thought, to know how much his friend hated her. To know how low was her value. It was as if Tommy Odds thought she was not a human being, as if her whiteness, the mystique of it, the *danger* of it, the historically *verboten* nature of it, encouraged him to attempt to destroy her without any feelings of guilt. It was so frightening a thought that she shook with it.

She had insisted on viewing them all as people who suffered without hatred; this was what intrigued her, made her like a child in awe of them. But she had not been thinking of individual lives, of young men like Tommy Odds whose thin defense against hatred broke down under personal assault. Revenge was his only comfort. And, she thought, on whom was such a man likely to take this revenge? Not on white men at large; certainly not. Not on the sheriff or the judge or the businessman sitting home over his drink. Not on the businessman's wife, because she *would* scream and put him away for good. He—Tommy Odds—had actually reached (and she understood this too well for her own comfort) an *improvement* in his choice of whom to punish, when he chose her. For, look at this: He had not, as black men had done foolishly for years, gotten drunk on the weekend and stabbed another black man to death. Nor had he married a black woman in order to possess, again erroneously, his own whipping post. Surely this was proof of a weird personal growth on Tommy's part. There were no longer any white boys, either, in the Movement, so that they could no longer be beaten up or turned, with guilty contempt, out into the street. That left her: a white woman without friends. A woman the white community already assumed was fucking every nigger in sight. Yes, Tommy Odds's logic—convoluted though it might be—was perfect.

But Truman didn't want her to leave. He would not give her money to leave even after she told him, hysterical finally, what had happened. He chose not to believe her.

Ask Tommy, she had cried. Just ask him! But if he did, she never knew.

"Why did you do it, man," Truman asked Tommy Odds.

"Because your woman ain't shit. She didn't even fight. She was just laying back waiting to give it up."

Lynne cried every night in her sleep. Truman could not bear it, so he did not usually come home. He slept on a couch in the center. His hand shot out and caught Odds at the base of the throat, which was black and scrawny, like the neck of a hen.

"She's better than you,*" he said, as Tommy Odds stretched his eyes wide, feigning fear. "You creep," said Truman, with a sneer, "you motherfucker. She felt sorry for you, because you lost your fucking arm."*

He raised his clenched fist underneath Odds's chin and, holding the collar of his shirt, rocked him back and forth, his feet nearly off the floor. It was like lifting a bag of loose, dirty laundry. "She felt sorry for you and look what you did."

Odds did not raise his hand to defend himself. He looked into Truman's eyes, and his own eyes were laughing. The laughter in them was like two melting ice cubes gleaming in a dish.

"You wish it was my fucking arm she felt sorry for."

"What do you mean, you son of a bitch?"

But Tommy Odds, tired now of being held in an awkward position, yanked himself out of Truman's grasp. He straightened his collar, tucked his shirt into his pants, extended his stub out from his side, like a turkey flapping a wing, and ran his fingers through his hair.

"Why don't you wise up," he said. "She didn't get involved with you *because of anything you lost."*

"Why don't you say what you mean!"

"I mean," said Tommy Odds mockingly, "it is true that you speaks French when you wants to impress folks, and it is true that you went to college, and it is true that you can draw and stuff and one time lived overseas for six months without pig feet or greens. But that ain't what won you Miss Lady Fair. Oh

nooooo . . . you're like a book she hadn't read; like a town she wanted to pass through; like a mango she wanted to taste because mangoes don't grow in her own yard. Boy, if you'd had an arm missing she probably would have kidnaped you a lot sooner than she did."

Truman wanted very much to destroy Tommy Odds. The impulse was overwhelming.

"Black men get preferential treatment, man, to make up for all we been denied. She ain't been fucking you, she's been atoning for her sins."

"That's not true," said Truman, sounding weak, even to himself.

"She felt sorry for me because I'm black, man," said Tommy Odds, and for the first time there was dejection in his voice. "The one thing that gives me some consolation in this stupid world, and she thinks she has to make up for it out of the bountifulness of her pussy." His voice hardened. "I should have killed her."

"No," said Truman, "no—"

Tommy Odds stood facing him. He looked terrible. Puny and exhausted and filthy. Dead. "Listen, man, you want to defend her. It's all right with me. I don't care, man. You want to beat me up," he said, "I'm ready, man. You want to kill me. Look, I won't even complain. You want me to go find you a gun? Or do you want to do it with your fists? Come on, man. Hit me. We'll feel better."

But Truman had already turned away.

And so Lynne sat alone, at home always now because she was afraid to go over to the center she had helped create. Afraid and ashamed and not even conscious enough of her own worth to be angry that she was ashamed. She counted the days until she was sure she was not pregnant. When she sold one of her poems—to an anthologist who wanted to document the Movement in poetry, and who wanted the white woman's point of view—she bought birth control pills. Enough for two months.

Because of what Tommy Odds had done Lynne locked her door, even to her friends Hedge and Altuna and Raymond.

They came back again and again. At first she looked at them from behind a window shade, ashamed and resentful of her fear. Eventually—from loneliness only—she opened the door and soon everything was, seemingly, back to normal. The boys were as courteous and shy as ever. Truman was not at home very much and when he was home he didn't speak to her. Some nights when she became lonely to the point of suicide, she played checkers with Alonzo, Altuna's brother, who worked at the scrap yard. A man who appeared completely unaware of the Movement and who never had any interest in voting, marching or anything else, he treated her with the stiff, sober courtesy of old-time Negroes. For his kindness, she invited him to sleep with her. In his gratitude, he licked her from her earlobes to her toes.

On Saturday nights her house became a place of music. She was protected now because she had a special friend in Alonzo. (Everyone seemed to understand that Truman no longer cared.) Men and women came to the house because they heard you could listen to records and dance and smoke reefers. But if she thought being Alonzo's friend was going to save her from other men she was wrong. They pleaded, they cajoled, they begged. And always, in refusing them, she saw their softening, earnest faces go rigid with hatred and she shivered, and began, over the months, to capitulate. She tried in vain to make them her friends, as Alonzo was. But they began to drive up, take her to bed (or on the floor, upside the wall), as if she were a prostitute, get up and leave. In public they did not speak to her.

Still, the women found out. They began to curse her and to threaten her, attacking her physically, some of them. And she began perversely to enjoy their misguided rage, to use it as acknowledgment of her irresistible qualities. It was during this time that whenever she found herself among black women, she found some excuse for taking down and combing her hair. As she swung it and felt it sweep the back of her waist, she imagined she possessed treasures they could never have.

She began to believe the men fucked her from love, not from hatred. For as long as they did not hate her she felt she could live. She could bear the hatred of her own father and mother, but not the hatred of black men. And when they no longer came to her—and she did not know why they did not—she realized she needed them. And then there were only Lynne and Truman and when her pills gave out she became pregnant with Camara, and finally took a bus to New York, where Welfare placed her in a one-room apartment near Avenue C.

Truman she had magnanimously sent back to Meridian, at his insistence.

On Giving Him Back to His Own

The subway train rushed through the tunnel screeching and sending out sparks like a meteor. And Lynne would not sit down while it flew. Ninety-sixth Street flashed by, then 125th, then there was a screaming halt, a jolt as the car resisted the sudden stop, and the doors slid back with a rubbery thump. The graffiti, streaked on the walls in glowing reds and glaring yellows, did not brighten at all the dark damp cavern of the station.

"Legs, man," a boy whispered to his comrade, pausing on the oily stairs as she passed.

"Right on," he was answered.

She darted up and around people as she rushed upward to the air, thinking, with a part of her brain, that fresh air was certainly what she needed. Nor did she notice any longer that nowhere in the city was the air fresh. Only sometimes, when she took Camara to the park, and even then . . . She turned left as she emerged from the subway, trotting now on her dancer's legs, thinking of herself already in the apartment, the neat space of quiet light and white walls where Truman worked night and day on the century's definitive African-American masterpieces.

They would not fight, she warned herself. She would be lady-like and precise and he would respond to her cry of help for their child.

"Our daughter has been hurt," she would say, with the sweet desperation of Loretta Young. Or, "I mean," slouching with her hands in her pockets like Mia Farrow looking for a tacos stand, "the kid's been beat *up.*" Or, looking as if about to choke on her own vomit, like Sandy Dennis, but *cool,* "There's been. . . . an accident. Our child. Attacked. Oh, can't you hurry?" And Truman would respond with all the old tenderness that she knew.

She took the stairs two at a time, her hair streaming and unwashed, her face feeling sooty, until she stood in front of his door. Apartment 3-C. Truman Held, Artist.

It was only then that she thought to rest, to compose herself, to suck in her stomach, which felt flabby and at the same time inflated. She was no longer a size seven. This mattered, the longer she huddled there.

Even when Truman was leaving her she had been conscious of her size, her body, from years of knowing how he compared it to the bodies of black women. "Black women let themselves go," he said, even as he painted them as magnificent giants, breeding forth the warriors of the new universe. "They are so *fat,*" he would say, even as he sculpted a "Big Bessie Smith" in solid marble, caressing her monstrous and lovely flanks with an admiring hand.

Her figure then, supple from dancing, was like a straw in the wind, he said, her long hair a song of lightness—untangled, glistening and free. And yet, in the end, he had stopped saying those things, at least out loud. It was as if the voluptuous black bodies, with breasts like melons and hair like a crown of thorns, reached out—creatures of his own creation—and silenced his tongue. They began to claim him. When she walked into a room where he painted a black woman and her heaving, pulsating, fecund body, he turned his work from her, or covered it up, or ordered her out of the room.

She had loved the figures at first—especially the paintings of women in the South—the sculptures, enduring and triumphant in spite of everything. But when Truman changed, she had, too. Until she did not want to look at the women, although many of them she knew, and loved. And by then she was willing to let him go. Almost. So worthless did the painted and sculptured women make her feel, so sure was she that Truman, having fought through his art to the reality of his own mother, aunts, sisters, lovers, to their beauty, their greatness, would naturally seek them again in the flesh.

He would always be Camara's father, he said, repeatedly. He would never forsake *her.* White-looking though she was.

She rang the bell, long and insistently.

"Why the fuck don't he answer," she muttered. She pulled her jacket close around her body and pressed her arms against her sides. She heard the crunch and crackle of a bag of fried plantains being crushed in her pocket. Her other pocket contained a small rubber ball, some string, a sliver of cheese Camara had slipped in when she wasn't looking. Pennies that she'd collected from Camara's clothing at the hospital rattled in her purse.

A light across her toes preceded the opening of the door. Truman, his hair in two dozen small braids, looked out at her.

"It's me," she said, trying to smile. Smiling, in fact.

He did not throw open the door.

"Who is it, True?" a voice from the bedroom beyond wafted out. Lynne felt a tingling at the base of her neck, like a rash trying to break through the skin.

"Just a minute," he called back. Warily he loosened the chain. But when Lynne moved forward she bumped into him. He was moving out, pulling the door closed behind him.

"Shit," she said, stepping back. "Why don't you just tell Meridian it's me. We don't have any secrets, do we?"

"What do you want, Lynne?"

"Really," she said, still smiling a silly too-bright smile, "I thought I would have a chance to come in and tell you in style, if not exactly in comfort. I'm thirsty, got any sodas?" She knew she was acting like a silly bitch—one of his favorite, most benign descriptions of her, but she couldn't help it. How could she tell him that his six-year-old daughter—

whom he insisted on nick-naming Princess (tacky, *tacky*, she'd told him)—had been attacked by a grown man and was now lying nearly dead in the hospital. How could she tell him she just needed his fucking support, standing on a stairwell in the dark?

"It's not Meridian," Truman said. He reached into his jeans and brought out his little cigars. She had leaned against the wall, thinking—like the silly bitch she was—but I gave you up for Meridian. For black, brown-skinned Meridian, with her sweet colored-folks' mouth, and her heroic nigger-woman hair.

"I am *not* going to make a scene," she mumbled warningly to herself. "We're not going to fight like we usually do."

"Of course we're not going to fight," said Truman, his artist's eye taking her in from white parched face and cracked lips to the thick unstylish bulges she thought she was hiding under her coat.

"Anybody I know?" she said, with a laugh, as faked as her smile.

"No."

"I am not going to make a scene," she began again. "We're not going to fight. . . ." But before he could stop her she had pushed the door open and stood halfway across the room staring into the eyes of a tiny blonde girl in a tiny, tiny slip that was so sheer she had time to notice—before Truman swung her around—that the girl's pubic hair was as blonde as the hair on her head.

"Will you tell me why you come up here

bothering me? Or is this just some more of your shit?"

Just some more, she wanted to assure him. But she couldn't speak. She stood between Truman and the girl and looked from one to the other. The girl said "I—" and Truman cut her off.

"Go back in there," he ordered, twisting his head.

"But I—" the girl began again.

And Lynne began to laugh. She laughed and laughed and laughed. She laughed so hard she got stitches in her side. Then she stopped. She felt that tingle again at the base of her throat.

"Why is it I don't ever learn *nothing*?" she asked. "Why is it that everybody in the fucking *world* learns what makes it go round before I do? Am I just dumb, or what? What do you reckon, Miss?" She turned to the girl and reached out her hand.

"Don't shut up, sugah," she said. "Talk. I wants to hear Miz Scarlet talk." Truman moved close to her and she waved him away.

"Troo-*mun*?" the girl said, stepping around Lynne as if she had lice. But Truman had turned his back. He stood by the window smoking, looking down into the street.

"Shoot," said Lynne, and she noticed her voice was now completely changed; she did not sound at all like herself. "Don't pay that ol' sucker no mind. Talk. You silly bitch yourself!"

And then the girl's words, melodious as song, southerly as trade winds, came softly out, like the bewildered mewling of a cat.

"Why, what's *wrong*?" drawled the girl, and the pine scents of Alabama, the magnolia smell of Georgia and Mississippi floated out of her mouth. "We've been livin' together for two months. Soon as—Truman says soon as he sells some more of his paintings we're goin' to be married. I don't need to tell you how I expect my folks to take it. . . ." A gleam of conspiracy had the nerve to be observed in her eye. She raised a delicate hand to point to all of Lynne's lost and grieved old friends gazing down serenely from the walls. "Aren't they *great*?" she innocently asked.

Two Women

And then there was the part Meridian knew, because she had been the first person Truman sent for when Camara died. Lynne didn't know what had happened to Scarlet O'Hara. It was Meridian they both needed, and it was Meridian who was, miraculously, there.

"Help me through this shit," Truman had said when Meridian walked off the bus into his arms. And she had, but she had also tried to help Lynne.

She had spent a month shuttling between his lovely bright studio uptown (where a painting of her own face surprised her on every wall) to Lynne's tiny hovel downtown. Between them they had drained her dry. She could not even think of that miserable month, later, without seeing it as a story told about someone else. She remembered the last days especially as one of those silent movies with Meridian Hill the poor star, dashing in and out of subways, cooking meals, listening to monologues thickened with grief, being pulled into bed—by Lynne, who held on to her like a child afraid of the dark—and by Truman, who almost drowned his body with her own, stuffing her flesh into his mouth as if he literally starved for her. It was then that her feeling for Truman returned, but it was not sexual. It was love totally free of possessiveness or contempt. It was love that purged all thought of blame from her too accurate memory. It was forgiveness.

Lynne remembered Meridian's last evening with her. "What time is Truman coming?" she had asked, because she did not want to be there when he arrived.

"He ought to be here any minute," said Lynne, beginning to rock, and feeling herself, in the rocking, growing old.

As they sat they watched a television program. One of those Southern epics about the relationship of the Southern white man to madness, and the closeness of the Southern black man to the land. It did not delve into the women's problems, black or white. They sat, companionable and still in their bathrobes, watching the green fields of the South and the indestructible (their word) faces of black people much more than they watched the madness. For them, the madness was like a puzzle they had temporarily solved (Meridian would sometimes, in the afternoons, read poems to Lynne by Margaret Walker, and Lynne, in return, would attempt to cornrow Meridian's patchy short hair), they hungered after more intricate and enduring patterns. Sometimes they talked, intimately, like sisters, and when they did not they allowed the television to fill the silences.

There was a scene on the television of a long, shady river bank and people—mothers and fathers, children, grandparents—almost elegantly fishing, and then the face, close up, of a beautiful young black man with eyes as deceptively bright as dying stars. Now that he had just about won the vote, he was saying, where was he to get the money to pay for his food? Looks like this whole Movement for the vote and to get into motels was just to teach him that everything in this country, from the vote to motels, had to be changed. In fact, he said, looks like what he needed was a gun.

To them both this was obvious. That the country was owned by the rich and that the rich must be relieved of this ownership before "Freedom" meant anything was something so basic to their understanding of America they felt naive even discussing it. Still, the face got to them. It was the kind of face they had seen only in the South. A face in which the fever of suffering had left an immense warmth, and the heat of pain had lighted a candle behind the eyes. It sought to understand, to encompass everything, and the struggle to live honorably and understand everything at the same time, to allow for every inconsistency in nature, every weird possibility and personality, had given it a weary serenity that was so entrenched and stable it could be mistaken for stupidity. It made them want to love. It made them want to weep. It made them want to cry out to the young man to run away, or at least warn him about how deeply he would be hurt. It made them homesick.

"We got any peaches?"

"I'd settle for a pine tree limb."

And Meridian and Lynne got up, rummaged around the apartment, looking for some traces of their former Southern home. Lynne found her Turkey Walk quilt and spread it over her knees.

In the small, shabby apartment there were mementos of other places, other things. There was, for example, a child's day bed folded up in a corner of the living room. Toys—if you opened the closet door too quickly—fell on your head. Tiny scuffed white shoes were still hiding—one of them, anyhow—under the headboard of the bed. Small worn dresses, ripped, faded or in good repair, hung on nails in a small back room.

The absence of the child herself was what had finally brought them together. Together they had sustained a loss not unlike the loss of Martin Luther King or Malcolm X or George Jackson. They grieved more because the child, Camara (after Camara Laye, the African novelist who, of course, did not know of her existence, but whose book *The Radiance of the King* had struck a responsive chord in Lynne), had been personally known, had been small—six years old—and had died after horrible things were done to her. They knew her suffering did not make her unique; but knowing that crimes of passion or hatred against children are not considered unique in a society where children are not particularly valued, failed to comfort them.

They waited for the pain of Camara's death to lessen. They waited to ask forgiveness of each other. They waited until they could talk again. And they waited for Truman, Camara's father, to come to his wife who had faced her tragedy as many a welfare mother before her had done: She had turned to pills, excesses of sex (or excesses of abstinence; Meridian wasn't sure which), and she had wandered back to the South, where she and Truman—she seemed fuzzily to remember—had for a short time been happy. And she had had a public mental breakdown. The first that many of the people there had seen. (For when their own relatives regularly freaked out a breakdown was not what it was called. Breakdown was, after all, different from *broke down*—as in "So-and-so just broke *down.*" Usually at a funeral.)

"I want to tell you something," said Meridian. "I tried very hard not to hate you. And I think I always succeeded."

"It ain't easy not to hate the omnipresent honky woman," said Lynne.

"I agree."

Meridian's bags had not actually been unpacked. She collected her tights and toothbrush from the bathroom.

"Thanks, Meridian, for everything. I honestly don't know what I would have done without you."

"You would have had Truman," said Meridian.

"Ah, Truman," said Lynne. "The last thing that held us together is safely buried." And she bit her lip in an effort not to cry. "I guess I should be glad," she said. "I guess I should be thankful it's over. 'You can go home now,' is what Truman said to me. Like, this little flirtation of yours to find out how the other half lives is over now, so you can just take your sorry white ass home. Can't you just see me walking in on my folks: 'Hi, y'all, that black nigger I run off with done left me, my *mu*latto kid done died. I reckon I'm ready to go to graduate school.' Meridian," she said, looking up at her, "do you realize how fucked up everything *is*?"

"Yep," said Meridian.

"I can't go back home. I don't even have a home. I wouldn't go back if I could. I know white folks are evil and fucked up, I *know* they're doomed. But where does that leave me? I *know* I have feelings, like any other human being. Camara wasn't just some little black kid that got ripped off on the street. She was my *child.* I'd have to walk over my child's *grave* to go back, and I won't."

"I know," said Meridian.

Meridian had hugged her, she had hugged Meridian, and they had parted. Lynne had soon drifted into a kind of sleep, while thinking of the South.

Lynne

Yes, she had gone back to the South. Back to the small unpainted house. It was deserted, forlorn, an abandoned friend.

She did not stop to wonder if someone would charge breaking and entering. She pulled herself up on the porch, feeling glass beneath her feet, and tried first to look into a window. She could reach her hand right through, because some of the panes were gone. Then she tried the door. It was not locked: She had not wondered whether it would or would not be. She entered the house as she used to, stepping quickly over the raised door-jamb, stepping down, then reached out to flick on the light. It was not working, whether because the power had been shut off or not she did not care. It was dark. She felt, with her fingers sliding through cob-webs, over dust, for some familiar objects on a windowsill. Soon she lit the remains of a multicolored candle. The dust burned with a keen dry smell. The cot was there. She threw herself upon it, raising still more dust. She spread her scarf under her head, her cheek. She was more tired than hungry. She kicked off her shoes. Drew her coat over her. And fell asleep.

She slept the clock around, so that when she awoke it was still quite dark. She rose unsteadily, feeling in the moment of rising refreshed, not in need yet of the blue and orange pills in clear plastic phials in her bag. She put on her shoes easily in the darkness, her feet were cold, and moved over to the window. It was a night with clouds, gray and luminous clouds because the moon was behind them. Through the trees just off the porch she could almost see it. The yard was quiet, even the trees did not bow and whisper as she had remembered them doing. But maybe that was because it was not yet summer. It was not yet even spring, though here it seemed spring. After the long winter in the North, where winter winds still raged and snow had followed the bus as far as northern Tennessee, the air here was light and warm on her skin, a trifle moist; with something kissing, she thought, with that easy poetical association she did not admire in herself.

In that yard they had sat in July and August and other hot days, eating countless watermelons, sticky, cool, good, running juice making tracks down her arms. He had photographed her once eating watermelon, and the lines on her arms ruined the picture; they came through like inverted veins, as if some slimy thing had left a whitish scar that dug into the skin. In spite of this she had liked the picture. Her hair, as usual, was loose, coming to below her waist, black, without curl. Her eyes bright (also black, in the photograph, without their brown subtlety), bold, searching for the thumb that would press the camera button. No surprise. Waiting. So that now when she looked out at the steps she thought she might still be sitting there, unmoved by all that had happened over the years. Sitting there, slender still, her white face happily covered by a fake sheet of brown, glowing, she thought, with health; and in any case, hiding the sickness.

The outhouse was not exactly out, but on the back porch. A dingy door-scratched room. Small, with only the essentials. She had lit another stub of a candle; no one seemed to have lived here since she left. There was still a shard of glass over the washbasin, like a triangle of flawed silver, the dust wiped off in a roll. The toilet gurgled and boiled before it worked. The posters had fallen away from the walls or rotted, but when she held her candle up to one she saw the grayed outline of hundreds of marching forms, though underneath this faded picture the words had been completely eroded away. It was as if the marchers moved through some ghostly, unreal place, specters themselves and not in the least afraid, apprehensive about what would happen when they floated off the picture, off the wall, into a place even more dead, more final.

She was moved to peel and eat an orange. Slowly. Sitting with her feet tucked under her, the candle on the floor, flickering with the small breezes that blew through the paneless window. In her sack she carried oranges, three apples, a triangle of cheese from the delicatessen: where the owners had recognized her and frozen up. She had stood smiling in the irritating way she had (the smile was even irritating to her, but she still used it) when she confronted bigots who also thought they owned her. They did not quite fling the food at her, across the counter, as they had done in the early days, when she would come in with one, maybe two, black men, or women. Or when she was beginning to show her pregnancy.

In the beginning she had actually been able to hear the intake of their breaths: the matronly woman who stood at the cash register, the younger woman who stood over the black cooks in the kitchen, the youngish man who, in the end (by the time Camara was ready to be born), spoke kindly to her, but with a kind of fear of her, like a fear for his own life, his precarious safety. She snatched her money up, looking steadily at all three of them, letting her eyes fudge them. They made her conscious, heavily, of her Jewishness, when, in fact, they wanted to make her feel her whiteness. And, beyond her whiteness, the whiteness that now engulfed this family (originally, she heard, from New York) like a shroud.

In the early days she would drop in for German beer with her black friends and the eye exchanges, a struggle of which her friends were completely unaware, would go on furiously between her and the three shopkeepers. The youngish man, already balding, his skin sallow from hanging there slicing salami week after week, could, by and by, speak quite plainly with his eyes. He said: We do not want you. Still, come back to us. It is not yet too late. (This was before she became pregnant.) They said: Have you found? Have you found? Her own eyes said to the women with their Southern-style, contrived, hornet-nest hair: You are wasted. Wasted. Surrounded by exotic foods! To the youngish balding man her eyes said: Yes! Yes! I have found. I am happy. Why do you think I glow this way? Idiot. Weakling. Slicer of salami. No-sex. Come back to you? Worm.

You are crazy. And what would you do if I did come back? Set me to wrapping pastrami? To fishing for pickles? Shithead. Unliving creature. Maker of money. Slicer of Salami. Baker of Challah!

Never once did they ask her what she was. And to them she spoke good finishing school English. It was just that they knew, as she knew about them. That they were transplanted, as they had always been, to a place where they fit like extra toes on a foot. Where they were trusted by no one, exploited, when possible, by anyone with political ambitions. Where they lived in a delicatessen, making money hand over fist because they could think of nothing more exciting to do with their lives. Making money to buy houses—garish, large, separate—outside the city. Making money to send their Elaines and Davids to law and medical school, without a word of official Hebrew, except when they visited in synagogues in the North where they also felt like strangers.

Goyim flitted in and out of the delicatessen, reeking of Southern tolerance and charm, like knife edges the forced smiles, the appreciation (genuine) of the food. Unusual, exotic, excellent. A change from pecan pie and gumbo eaten with a tall glass of ginger ale or Tom Collins.

She watched them over the years she lived in the town (because she would shop there, even though it was expensive and she had little money), and even watched the outside of the delicatessen when they closed it after the local synagogue was bombed. They were shocked, the papers said. Aghast at the bombing! She laughed at their naiveté. Laughed at their precarious "safety."

Laughed with such bitter contempt that she could not speak to a Southern Jew without wanting to hit him or her.

The cheese, a tin of Danish camembert, melted like butter on her tongue . . . .

The taste of the cheese brought her back, though she kept her head against the back of her chair, her eyes closed. She sat up, opened her eyes, looked at Meridian who had fallen asleep, and sprang to her feet, yawning loudly.

"Black folks aren't so special," she said. "I hate to admit it. But they're not."

"Maybe," said Meridian, as if she had been wide awake all along, "the time for being special has passed. Jews are fighting for Israel with one hand stuck in a crack in the Wailing Wall. Look at it this way, black folks and Jews held out as long as they could." Meridian rubbed her eyes.

"Good God, this is depressing," said Lynne. "It's even more depressing than knowing I want Truman back."

"That *is* depressing," said Meridian.

"Oh, I know he's not much," she said. "But he saved me from a fate worse than death. Because of him, I can never be as dumb as my mother was. Even if I practiced not knowing what the world is like, even if I lived in Scarsdale or some other weird place, and never had to eat welfare food in my life, I'd still *know*. By nature I'm not cut out to be a member of the oppressors. I don't like them; they make me feel guilty all the time. They're ugly and don't know poor people laugh at them and are just waiting to drag them out. No, Truman isn't much, but he's *instructional,*" said Lynne. "Besides," she continued, "nobody's perfect."

"Except white women," said Meridian, and winked.

"Yes," said Lynne, "but their time will come."

Ending

No foreign sky protected me,
no stranger's wing shielded my face.
I stand as witness to the common lot,
survivor of that time, that place.

—Akhmatova: "Requiem"

Free at Last

A DAY IN APRIL, 1968

Long before downtown Atlanta was awake, she was there beside the church, her back against the stone. Like the poor around her, with their meager fires in braziers against the April chill, she had brought fried chicken wrapped in foil and now ate it slowly as she waited for the sun. The nearby families told their children stories about the old days before black people marched, before black people voted, before they could allow their anger or even their exhaustion to show. There were stories, too, of Southern hunts for coons and 'possums among the red Georgia hills, and myths of strong women and men, Indian and black, who knew the secret places of the land and refused to be pried from them. As always they were dressed in their very Sunday best, and were resigned; on their arms the black bands of crepe might have been made of iron.

They were there when the crowd began to swell, early in the morning. Making room, giving up their spots around the entrance to the church, yet still pressing somehow forward, with their tired necks extended, to see, just for a moment, just for a glimpse, the filled coffin.

They were there when the limousines began to arrive, and there when the family, wounded, crept up the steps, and there when the senators running for President flashed by, and there when the horde of clergy in their outdone rage stomped by, and there when the movie stars glided, as if slowly blown, into the church, and there when all these pretended not to see the pitiable crowd of nobodies who hungered to be nearer, who stood outside throughout the funeral service (piped out to them like scratchy Muzak) and shuffled their feet in their too tight shoes, and cleared their throats repeatedly against their tears and all the same helplessly cried.

Later, following the casket on its mule-drawn cart, they began to sing a song the dead man had loved. "I come to the gar-den *alone*. . . . While the dew is still on the *ro*-ses. . . ." Such an old favorite! And neutral. The dignitaries who had not already slipped away—and now cursed the four-mile walk behind the great dead man—opened their mouths eagerly in genial mime. Ahead of Meridian a man paraded a small white poodle on a leash. The man was black, and a smiler. As he looked about him a tooth encased in patterned gold sparkled in his mouth. On the dog's back a purple placard with white lettering proclaimed "I have a dream."

Then she noticed it: As they walked, people began to engage each other in loud, even ringing, conversation. They inquired about each other's jobs.

They asked after members of each other's families. They conversed about the weather. And everywhere the call for Coca-Colas, for food, rang out. Popcorn appeared, and along their route hot-dog stands sprouted their broad, multicolored umbrellas. The sun came from behind the clouds, and the mourners removed their coats and loosened girdles and ties. Those who had never known it anyway dropped the favorite song, and there was a feeling of relief in the air, of liberation, that was repulsive.

Meridian turned, in shame, as if to the dead man himself.

"It's a black characteristic, man," a skinny black boy tapping on an imaginary drum was saying. "We don't go on over death the way whiteys do." He was speaking to a white couple who hung on guiltily to every word.

Behind her a black woman was laughing, laughing, as if all her cares, at last, had flown away.

Questions

"I'm afraid I won't be able to live up to what is required of me—by history, by economics. . . ."

"But there's so much you can give, other than being able to kill. That should be self-evident."

"It isn't though."

"I used to raise my arm and shout, 'Death to honkies,' too," said Truman, "but I understood I didn't really mean it. Not *really.* Not like the men who attacked the police during the riots. I thought of what it would be like to kill, when I thought I was going to be drafted. In the army, killing would be all right, I supposed. Since I wasn't drafted, it seemed useless to think about it.

"In the army you would simply kill to keep yourself alive. Revolutionary killing is systematic. You line people up who have abused you, as a group, and you simply eradicate them, like you would eradicate a disease."

"A disease with faces, with children . . . human voices."

"Yes, but a disease nonetheless." To Truman the

discussion was academic, so he could state his points neatly. "By the way," he now said, "do you think you *could* kill anyone, lined up before you like so much diphtheria or smallpox? Or cancer?" Although, to Truman, the rich were a cancer on the world, he would not mind being rich himself.

Meridian laughed, the stubborn ambivalence of her nature at last amusing her. "Sometimes I'm positive I could. Other times I'm just as sure I could not. And even if I felt sure I could do it all the time I still couldn't *know*, could I, until the occasion for killing someone presented itself? Besides," she said, "I don't trust revolutionaries enough to let them choose who should be killed. *I* would probably end up on the wrong side of the firing squad, myself."

"No one would ask killing of *you*," said Truman.

"Because I'm a woman?"

"Oh, Christ," said Truman, "because you're obviously not cut out for it. You're too sensitive. One shot and even though you missed you'd end up a basket case."

"That's true," said Meridian, "but do you think that has anything to do with it? I don't. I mean, I think that all of us who want the black and poor to have equal opportunities and goods in life will have to ask ourselves how we stand on killing, even if no one else ever does. Otherwise we will never know—in advance of our fighting—how much we are willing to give up."

"Suppose you found out, without a doubt, that you could murder other people in a just cause, what would you do? Would you set about murdering them?"

"Never alone," said Meridian. "Besides, revolution would not begin, do you think, with an act of murder—wars might begin in that way—but with teaching."

"Oh yes, *teaching*," said Truman, scornfully.

"I would like to teach again," said Meridian. "I respect it, when it's done right. After all, people want to be taught how to live. . . ."

"And do you think you could teach them?"

"I don't know. I imagine good teaching as a circle of earnest people sitting down to ask each other meaningful questions. I don't see it as a handing down of answers. So much of what passes for teaching is merely a pointing out of what items to want."

"Meridian," Truman said. "Do you realize no one is thinking about these things any more? Revolution was the theme of the sixties: Medgar, Malcolm, Martin, George, Angela Davis, the Panthers, people blowing up buildings and each other. But all that is gone now. I am, myself, making a statue of Crispus Attucks for the Bicentennial. We're here to stay: the black and the poor, the Indian, and now all those illegal immigrants from the West Indies who adore America just the way it is."

"Then you think revolution, like everything else in America, was reduced to a fad?"

"Of course," said Truman. "The leaders were killed, the restless young were bought off with antipoverty jobs, and the clothing styles of the poor were copied by Seventh Avenue. And you *know* how many middle-class white girls from Brooklyn started wearing kinky hair."

"But don't you think the basic questions raised by King and Malcolm and the rest still exist? Don't you think people, somewhere deep inside, are still attempting to deal with them?"

"No," said Truman.

"Is there no place in a revolution for a person who *cannot* kill?" asked Meridian, obviously not believing him.

"Why do you drive yourself crazy over these questions?" asked Truman, leaning over her. "When the time comes, trust yourself to do the right thing."

"The 'right' thing? Or merely the thing that will save my life?"

"Don't nitpick."

"No. Don't you see, what you mean is that I should trust myself to do the 'correct' thing. But I've always had trouble telling the 'correct' thing from the 'right' thing. The right thing is never to kill. I will always believe that. The correct thing is to kill when killing is necessary. And it sometimes is, I *know* that."

She could not help struggling with these questions. Just as Truman could not help thinking such struggle useless. In the end people did what they had to do to survive. They acquiesced, they rebelled, they sold out, they shot it out, or they simply drifted with the current of the time, whatever it was. And they didn't endanger life and limb agonizing over what they would lose, which was what separated them from Meridian.

It was a small white house, freshly painted by the black community, with green shutters and a green door. It sat on a bank over a dirt street as did all the other houses. The "street" was a road filled with ruts, and on each side were shallow gullies thick with weeds and straggly yellow flowers. From the road the house was almost entirely hidden by a fence made of hog wire that had slowly, over the years, become covered with running vines which revealed themselves each summer to be blue and purple morning glories and orange and yellow honeysuckle, and in the winter there was a green and leafy ivy. The gate, too, was vine-covered and opened with a rusty iron clasp. From the road, only the chimney could be seen, and a ribbon of black roof. The yard sloped down in back to a large ditch that ran the length of the street, which the residents of the area called, with impotent bitterness, "the pool." When it rained, children were forbidden to play outside because the water in the pool could rise silently as a thief until it covered the head of a three-year-old.

But the children loved to play in the pool when the weather was hot and would sneak behind their houses to wade in it. The public white swimming pool, having been ordered, by the federal government, opened to blacks, was closed by city officials who were all rich and white and who had, moreover, their own private swimming pools in their own back yards. There had never been a public swimming pool for blacks, few of whom, consequently, knew how to swim.

Flooding was especially bad in the spring and fall because the heaviest rains came then. But in addition to this, the same city officials who had closed the public swimming pool had erected a huge reservoir very near the lower-lying black neighborhood. When the waters of the reservoir rose from the incessant rains, the excess was allowed to drain off in any direction It would. Since this was done without warning, the disobedient children caught wading in the pool were knocked off their feet and drowned.

Whenever this happened, as it did every year, the people of the community habitually cried and took gifts of fruit and fried chicken to the bereaved family. The men stood about in groups, cursing the mayor and the city commissioner and the board of aldermen, whom they, ironically, never failed to refer to as "the city fathers." The women would sit with the mother of the lost child, recall their own lost children, stare at their cursing husbands—who could not look back at them—and shake their heads.

It was Meridian who had led them to the mayor's office, bearing in her arms the bloated figure of a five-year-old boy who had been stuck in the sewer for two days before he was raked out with a grappling hook. The child's body was so ravaged, so grotesque, so disgusting to behold, his own mother had taken one look and refused to touch him. To the people who followed Meridian it was as if she carried a large bouquet of long-stemmed roses. The body might have smelled just that sweet, from the serene, set expression on her face. They had followed her into a town meeting over which the white-haired, bespectacled mayor presided, and she had placed the child, whose body was beginning to decompose, beside his gavel. The people had turned with her and followed her out. They had been behind her when, at some distance from the center of town, she had suddenly buckled and fallen to the ground.

When she was up again they came to her and offered her everything, including the promise that they would name the next girl child they had after her. Instead she made them promise they would learn, as their smallest resistance to the murder of their children, to use the vote.

At first the people laughed nervously. "But that's nothing," these people said, who had done nothing before beyond complaining among themselves and continually weeping. "People will laugh at us because that is not radical," they said, choosing to believe radicalism would grow over their souls, like a bright armor, overnight.

There were two rooms. In one, a hot plate, a table and a battered chair (brought by the neighbors when they brought the food and the cow), and in the other, where Meridian slept, only her sleeping bag on the floor, some toilet articles on a windowsill (which Truman had overlooked before) and a jar of dried wildflowers in a green wine bottle placed in a corner. And, of course, the letters.

Truman was always looking for Meridian, even when he didn't know it. He was always finding her, as if she pulled him by an invisible string. But though he always found her, she was never what he expected. This time would not be different.

She would not ride in his new green car. "That's a pretty car," she said, "but I prefer to walk."

"Ten years ago," said Truman, "when your kind of protest was new and still fashionable, we *had* to walk. Now we can ride. Or is riding in new cars part of what you are protesting?"

"I suppose it is something like that," she said.

"Then why not go all out," he said, "and put rocks in your shoes?"

Camara

Sometime after the spring of '68, Meridian began going, irregularly, to church. The first time, a hot Sunday in June, she had stood in the doorway of a store across the street, watching the people arrive. They drove up in shiny cars of green and brown and black, and emerged well dressed, powdered and brushed, hair glistening, handbags of patent leather, the men formal and cool in dark brown, gray or black suits, the women colorful in dresses of bright pink, yellow and pastel blue, with flowers.

She felt a certain panic, watching them. They seemed so unchanged by everything that had happened to them. True, the church was not like the ones of her childhood; it was not shabby or small. It was large, of brick, with stained-glass windows of yellow and brown squares, and no red or blue. An imposing structure; and yet it did not reach for the sky, as cathedrals did, but settled firmly on the ground. She was aware of the intense heat that closed around the church and the people moving slowly, almost grandly up the steps, as if into an ageless photograph. And she, standing across the street, was not part of it. Rather, she sensed herself an outsider, as a single eye behind a camera that was aimed from a corner of her youth, attached now only because she watched. If she were not there watching, the scene would be exactly the same, the "picture" itself never noticing that the camera was missing.

Each Sunday, for several weeks, she chose a different church. Finally, for no reason she was sure of, she found herself in front of a large white church, Baptist (with blue and red in its stained windows, perhaps that was what drew her), and she sucked in her breath and went up the steps and inside. The church was nearly full and an usher—a quiet young boy, strong-limbed but *contained* in his somber blue suit—showed her to a seat near the entrance. It was unreal to her that people still *came*, actually got out of bed on Sunday morning and came, to church; and she stared up at them as they passed, her mouth slightly open.

A dark, heavy man with bulging red eyes—eyes sad or mean she could not tell—shuffled by her bench and went up to the pulpit, which drew her attention to the small group of people assembled there. A humble-looking creature in a snuff brown suit brought from behind the altar a large photograph of a slain martyr in the Civil Rights struggle. Two tiny black girls promptly rose and placed tall vases of lilies—white and unblemished (their green stalks waxy and succulent)—on either side.

She stood as the people began to sing a once quite

familiar song. But now she could not remember the words; they seemed stuck in some pinched-over groove in her memory. She stared at the people behind the altar, distractedly clutching the back of the bench in front of her. She did not want to find right then whatever it was she was looking for. She had no idea, really, what it was. And yet, she was *there.* She opened her mouth and attempted to sing, but soon realized it was the melody of the song she remembered, not the words, because these words sounded quite new to her.

The man with the red eyes whispered to the people around him, mopping his face and neck with a handkerchief that showed snowy against his glistening skin. One of the men rose and asked someone to lead them in prayer. The man who came forward did not kneel. He stood straight, his shoulders back, his face stern before the congregation. He said they were glad to have this opportunity to be with one another again. He said they were thankful to be alive and to be, for the most part, healthy, and holding together as a community and as families. He said he was thankful they could count on each other in times of trouble. He said he would not pray any longer because there was a lot of work for the community to do. He sat down.

This prayer was followed by another song that was completely foreign to Meridian, whose words were completely hidden from her by the quite martial melody. It seemed to Meridian that this was done deliberately; in any case, her consciousness was no longer led off after a vain search for words she could not recall, but began instead to slowly merge itself with the triumphant forcefulness of the oddly death-defying music.

"Let the martial songs be written," she found herself quoting Margaret Walker's famous poem; "let the dirges disappear!" She started and looked quickly around her. The people looked exactly as they had ever since she had known black churchgoing people, which was all her life, but they had changed the music! She was shocked.

The minister—in his thirties, dressed in a neat black suit and striped tie of an earlier fashion—spoke in a voice so dramatically like that of Martin Luther King's that at first Meridian thought his intention was to dupe or to mock. She glanced about to see if anyone else showed signs of astonishment or derision. But every face on her bench looked forward stoically, and even the chattering young men across the aisle from her did not seem perturbed. Her first impulse had been to laugh bitterly at the pompous, imitative preacher. But she began, instead, to listen. David and Goliath were briefly mentioned, to illustrate a point. Then the preacher launched into an attack on President Nixon, whom he called "Tricky Dick"! He looked down on the young men in the audience and forbade them to participate in the Vietnam war. He told the young women to stop looking for husbands and try to get something useful in their heads. He told the older congregants that they should be ashamed of the way they let their young children fight their battles for them. He told them they were cowardly and pathetic when they sent their small children alone into white neighborhoods to go to school. He abused the black teachers present who did not, he said, work hard enough to teach black youth because they obviously had no faith in them.

It struck Meridian that he was deliberately imitating King, that he and all his congregation *knew* he was consciously keeping that voice alive. It was like a *play.* This startled Meridian; and the preacher's voice—not his own voice at all, but rather the voice of millions who could no longer speak—wound on and on along its now heated, now cool, track. God was not mentioned, except as a reference.

She was suddenly aware that the sound of the "ah-mens" was different. Not muttered in resignation, not shouted in despair. No one bounced in his seat. No one even perspired. Just the "ah-mens" rose clearly, unsentimentally, and with a firm tone of "We are fed up."

When the red-eyed man rose there was a buzzing throughout the church. The preacher introduced him as the father of the slain man whose picture was flanked by the white lilies. Yes, now that he was introduced, Meridian remembered him. When his son was killed he had gone temporarily insane. Meridian had read about it in the paper. He had wrecked his own house with an ax, swinging until, absolutely, profoundly silent and blank, he had been carried out of the state and placed in a sanitarium. He had returned red-eyed and heavier and deadly calm—still taking tranquilizers, it was said, and thinking (the people whispered, hoped) of running for office. But this had not materialized.

He lived peacefully in the ruins of his wrecked house, his sanity coming back—unwelcomed—for days it a time. Then he bellowed out his loss. At other times he talked, in his normally reserved, rather ironic voice, to his wife and other children who were already dead (lost previously in a fire). His martyred son was all the family he had. He had boasted when the boy was younger, that his son—slender, black, as gentle and graceful as his mother had been, with her precious small hands—would be his bulwark, his refuge, when he grew old. He had not understood when his son chose struggle. He had understood even less when his son began to actually fight, to talk of bullets, of bombs, of revolution. For his talk alone (as far as his father knew, or believed, or wanted to know) they had killed him. And to his father—on sane days, doped to the gills with tranquilizers (because it was true, he ate them by the handfuls)—it still made no sense. He had thought that somehow, the power of his love alone (and how rare even he knew it was!) would save his son. But his love—selfless, open, a kissing, touching love—had only made his son strong enough to resist everything that was not love. Strong, beloved, knowing through his father's eyes his own great value, he had set out to change the ways of the world his father feared. And they had murdered him.

His father knew the beauty of his son's soul, as a jeweler knows the brilliance of the jewel beneath the stone, the gentleness at the heart of the warrior.

And it was for this loss he wept and detested life as capricious and unreasonable. And felt his life empty, and his heart deprived.

The people tried to be kind, as he had felt confident, even in his madness, they would be. It was a feeling he had shared with his son. For no matter how distrustful his son was of white people, rich people, or people who waged wars to destroy others, he had had absolute faith in the people among whom he had grown up. People like his father—who had been a simple mechanic, who owned his own small cluttered shop in which he did fine, proud, honest work—who could bear the weight of any oppression or any revolution as long as they knew they were together and believed the pain they suffered would come to a *righteous* end. The people would open themselves totally to someone else's personal loss, if it was allowed them to do so. But the father, insane half the time, and gladly so, did not allow closeness. He was, after a while, left alone with his memories and his ghosts.

It was only on occasions such as this, only on anniversaries of his son's death, that his presence was specifically requested, and he came out to the various schools and churches. He never looked at his son's picture, but would come and stand before the people because they, needing reminders, requested it of him. They accepted him then in whatever form he presented himself and knew him to be unpredictable. Today he stood for several minutes, his throat working, his eyes redder than ever, without tears. The congregation was quiet with reverence and an expectation that was already grateful, whatever he would give them. The words came from a throat that seemed stoppered with anxiety, memory, grief and dope. And the words, the beginning of a speech he had laboriously learned years ago for just such occasions as this when so much was asked of him, were the same that he gave every year. The same, exact, three. "My son died."

He stood there for several minutes more, on display. Sunk in his own memories, in confusion, in loss, then was led back gently to his seat, his large body falling heavily into his chair, his arms hanging limply, showing ashen palms to the crowd. And then there rose the sweet music, that received its inimitable *soul* from just such inarticulate grief as this, and a passing of the collection plate with the money going to the church's prison fund, and the preacher urged all those within his hearing to vote for black candidates on the twenty-third. And the service was over.

For a while, the congregation did not move. Meridian sat thinking of how much she had always disliked church. Whenever she was in a church, she felt claustrophobic, as if the walls were closing in. She had, even as a child, felt pity for the people who sat through the long and boring sermons listlessly fanning in the summer heat and hoping, vainly, she felt, for the best. The music she loved. Next to the music, she had liked only the stained-glass windows, when there were any, because the colored glass changed ordinary light into something richer, of gold and rose and mauve. It was restful and beautiful and inspired the reverence the sermons had failed to rouse. Thinking of the glass now she raised her head to look at the large stained-glass window across from her.

Instead of the traditional pale Christ with stray lamb there was a tall, broad-shouldered black man. He was wearing a brilliant blue suit through which the light swam as if in a lake, and a bright red tie that looked as if someone were pouring cherries down his chest. His face was thrown back, contorted in song, and sweat, like glowing diamonds, fell from his head. In one hand he held a guitar that was attached to a golden strap that ran over his shoulder. It was maroon, much narrower at one end than at the other, with amber buttons, like butterscotch kisses, on the narrow end. The other arm was raised above his head and it held a long shiny object the end of which was dripping with blood.

"What's that?" she asked the placid woman sitting next to her, who was humming and swatting flies and bopping her restless children, intermittently, on the head.

"What?" she turned kindly to Meridian and smiled in a charming and easygoing way. "Oh, *that.* One of our young artists did that. It's called "B.B., With Sword."

And what was Meridian, who had always thought of the black church as mainly a reactionary power, to make of this? What was anyone? She was puzzled that the music had changed. Puzzled that everyone in the congregation had anticipated the play. Puzzled that young people in church nowadays did not fall asleep. Perhaps it was, after all, the only place left for black people to congregate, where the problems of life were not discussed fraudulently and the approach to the future was considered communally, and moral questions were taken seriously.

She considered the face of the young man in the photograph as she was walking away. A face destroyed by clubs held by men. Now it would be nothing but the cracked bones, falling free as the skin rotted away, coming apart into the bottom of the casket; and the gentle fingers, all broken and crushed under the wheels of cars, would point directions no more. She would always love this young man who had died before she had a chance to know him. But how, she wondered, could she show her love for someone who was already dead?

There was a reason for the ceremony she had witnessed in the church. And, as she pursued this reason in her thoughts, it came to her. The people in the church were saying to the red-eyed man that his son had not died for nothing, and that if his son should come again they would protect his life with their own. "Look," they were saying, "we are slow to awaken to the notion that we are only as other women and men, and even slower to move in anger, but we are gathering ourselves to fight for and protect what your son fought for on behalf of us. If you will let us weave your story and your son's life and death into what we already know—into the songs, the sermons, the 'brother and sister'—we will soon be so angry we cannot help but move. Understand this," they were saying, "the church" (and Meridian knew they did not mean simply "church," as in Baptist, Methodist or whatnot, but rather communal spirit, togetherness, righteous convergence), "the music, the form of worship that has always sustained us, the kind of ritual you share with us, these are the ways to transformation that we know. We want to take this with us as far as we can."

In comprehending this, there was in Meridian's chest a breaking as if a tight string binding her lungs had given way, allowing her to breathe freely. For she understood, finally, that the respect she owed her life was to continue, against whatever obstacles, to live it, and not to give up any particle of it without a fight to the death, preferably *not* her own. And that this existence extended beyond herself to those around her because, in fact, the years in America had created them One Life. She had stopped, considering this, in the middle of the road. Under a large tree beside the road, crowded now with the cars returning from church, she made a promise to the red-eyed man herself: that yes, indeed she *would* kill, before she allowed anyone to murder his son again.

Her heart was beating as if it would burst, sweat poured down her skin. Meridian did not dare to make promises as a rule for fear some unforeseen event would cause her to break them. Even a promise to herself caused her to tremble with good faith. It was not a vain promise; and yet, if anyone had asked her to explain what it meant exactly she could not have told them. And certainly to boast about this new capacity to kill—which she did not, after all, admire—would be to destroy the understanding she had acquired with it. Namely, this: that even the contemplation of murder required incredible delicacy as it required incredible spiritual work, and the historical background and present setting must be right. Only in a church surrounded by the righteous guardians of the people's memories could she even approach the concept of retaliatory murder. Only among the pious could this idea both comfort and uplift.

Meridian's dedication to her promise did not remain constant. Sometimes she lost it altogether. Then she thought: I have been allowed to see how the new capacity to do anything, including kill, for our freedom—beyond sporadic acts of violence—is to emerge, and flower, but I am not yet at the point of being able to kill anyone myself, nor—except for the false urgings that come to me in periods of grief and rage—will I ever be. I am a failure then, as the kind of revolutionary Anne-Marion and her acquaintances were. (Though in fact she had heard of nothing revolutionary this group had done, since she left them ten summers ago. Anne-Marion, she knew, had become a well-known poet whose poems were about her two children, and the quality of the light that fell across a lake she owned.)

It was this, Meridian thought, I have not wanted to face, this that has caused me to suffer: I am not to belong to the future. I am to be left, listening to the old music, beside the highway. But then, she thought, perhaps it will be my part to walk behind the real revolutionaries—those who know they must spill blood in order to help the poor and the black and therefore go right ahead—and when they stop to wash off the blood and find their throats too choked with the smell of murdered flesh to sing, I will come forward and sing from memory songs they will need once more to hear. For it is the song of the people, transformed by the experience of each generation, that holds them together, and if any part of it is lost the people suffer and are without soul. If I can only do that, my role will not have been a useless one after all.

But at other times her dedication to her promise came back strongly. She needed only to see a starving child or attempt to register to vote a grown person who could neither read nor write. On those occasions such was her rage that she actually felt as if the rich and racist of the world should stand in fear of her, because she—though apparently weak and penniless, a little crazy and without power—was yet of a resolute and relatively fearless character, which, sufficient in its calm acceptance of its own purpose, could bring the mightiest country to its knees.

Travels

"Mama," a half-naked little boy called as they walked up to the porch, "it's some people out here, and one of 'em is that woman in the cap."

The wooden steps were broken and the porch sagged. In the front room a thin young man worked silently in a corner. In front of him was a giant pile of newspapers that looked as though they'd been salvaged from the hands of children who ate dinner over the funnies. Meridian and Truman watched the man carefully smooth out the paper, gather ten sheets, then twenty, and roll them into a log around which he placed a red rubber band. When he finished the "log" he stacked it, like a piece of wood, on top of the long pile of such "logs" that ran across one side of the poorly furnished, rather damp and smelly room.

Through the inner door he had a view of his wife—when he turned around to put the paper on the pile—lying on the bed. He nodded to them that they should enter his wife's room.

"How're you?" asked Meridian, as she and Truman looked about for chairs.

"Don't sit there," the woman said to Truman, who sat in a straight chair the young son brought. "You blocks my view of my husband."

"I'm sorry," said Truman, quickly moving.

"I'm feelin' a little better today," said the woman, "a little better." Her small black face was childlike, all bony points and big brown eyes that never left her husband's back.

"My husband Johnny went out and got me some venison and made me up a little stew. I think that's helping me to git my strength up some." She laughed, for no reason that her visitors could fathom. It was a soft, intimate chuckle, weak but as if she wanted them to understand she could endure whatever was wrong.

"Where did he get deer this time of year?" asked Truman.

"Don't tell anybody," the sick woman chuckled again, slyly, "but he went hunting out at one of those places where the sign says 'Deer Crossin'.' If we had a refrigerator we wouldn't need any more meat for the rest of the year. Johnny—" she began, showing all her teeth as one hand clutched the bedspread with the same intensity as her rather ghastly smile.

"Did you say somethin', Agnes?" asked Johnny, getting up from his chore with the newspapers and coming to stand at the foot of the bed. "You hongry again?"

"I gets full just lookin' at you, Sugah," said the sick woman coquettishly. "That's about the only reason I hate to die," she said, looking at her visitors for a split second, "I won't be able to see my ol' good-lookin' man."

"Shoot," said Johnny, going back to the other room.

"He used to be a worker at the copper plant, used to make wire. They fired him 'cause he wouldn't let the glass in front of his table stay covered up. You know in the plant they don't want the working folks to look at nothing but what's right on the table in front of them. But my Johnny said he wasn't no mule to be wearing blinders. He wanted to see a little bit of grass, a little bit of sky. It was bad enough being buried in the basement over there, but they wanted to even keep out the sun." She looked at her husband's back as if she could send her fingers through her eyes.

"What does he do with the newspapers?" asked Truman.

"Did you see how many he has?" asked the woman. "You should see the room behind this one. Rolled newspapers up to the ceiling. Half the kitchen is rolled newspapers." She chuckled hoarsely. "So much industry in him. Why, in the wintertime he and little Johnny will take them logs around to folks with fireplaces and sell'em for a nickel apiece and to colored for only three pennies."

"Hummm—" said Meridian. "Maybe we could help him roll a few while we're here. We just came by to ask if you all want to register to vote, but I think we could roll a few newspapers while you think about it."

"Vote?" asked the woman, attempting to raise

her voice to send the question to her husband. Then she lay back. "Go on in there and git a few pages," she said.

As soon as she touched the newspapers Meridian realized Johnny must have combed the city's garbage cans, trash heaps, and department store alleys for them. Many were damp and even slimy, as if fish or worse had been wrapped in them. She began slowly pressing the papers flat, then rolling them into logs.

The sick woman was saying, "I have this dream that if the Father blesses me I'll die the week before the second Sunday in May because I want to be buried on Mother's Day. I don't know why I want that, but I do. The pain I have is like my kidneys was wrapped in that straining gauze they use in dairies to strain milk, and something is squeezing and squeezing them. But when I die, the squeezing will stop. Round Mother's Day, if the merciful Father say so."

"Mama's goin' to heaven," said Johnny Jr., who came to roll the papers Meridian had smoothed.

"She's already sweet like an angel," said Meridian impulsively, rubbing his hair and picking away the lint, "like you."

"What good is the vote, if we don't own nothing?" asked the husband as Truman and Meridian were leaving. The wife, her eyes steadily caressing her husband's back, had fallen asleep, Johnny Jr. cuddled next to her on the faded chenille bedspread. In winter the house must be freezing, thought Truman, looking at the cracks in the walls; and now, in spring, it was full of flies.

"Do you want free medicine for your wife? A hospital that'll take black people through the front door? A good school for Johnny Jr. and a job no one can take away?"

"You know I do," said the husband sullenly.

"Well, voting probably won't get it for you, not in your lifetime," Truman said, not knowing whether Meridian intended to lie and claim it would.

"What *will* it get me but a lot of trouble," grumbled the husband.

"I don't know," said Meridian. "It may be useless. Or maybe it can be the beginning of the use of your voice. You have to get used to using your voice, you know. You start on simple things and move on. . . ."

"No," said the husband, "I don't have time for foolishness. My wife is dying. My boy don't have shoes. Go somewhere else and find somebody that ain't got to work all the time for pennies, like I do."

"Okay," said Meridian. Surprised, Truman followed as she calmly walked away.

"What's this here?" asked the husband ten minutes later as they came through his front door with two bags of food.

"To go with the venison." Meridian grinned.

"I ain't changed my mind," said the husband, with a suspicious peek into the bags.

And they did not see him again until the Monday

after Mother's Day, when he brought them six rabbits already skinned and ten newspaper logs; and under the words WILL YOU BE BRAVE ENOUGH TO VOTE in Meridian's yellow pad, he wrote his name in large black letters.

Treasure

They first saw the home of Miss Margaret Treasure through a landscape of smoke, while walking down a flat dirt road looking for people the census takers always missed. It was the middle of summer, hot as an oven, and sweat fell from their skin and evaporated before it hit the ground. On both sides of the road last year's cornstalks rustled in dry, lonely talk, and as the chimneys of the house wavered through the haze they saw a large black woman in a tight red dress hobbling toward them, a gasoline can in her hand. She was setting fire to the field.

Truman and Meridian stopped to watch her, and when the woman reached them she too stood still. She was obviously surprised to see them and dropped her gasoline can at Meridian's feet.

On the wide front porch of Miss Treasure's neat white house there was a gigantic mahogany bed with head and footboards towering over their heads. Meridian held the fat left hand of Miss Treasure and helped her down on it. Miss Treasure's tears dripped onto the snowy covering and had already washed pink grooves into the blackness of her skin.

"I got to burn this bed," said Miss Treasure, slamming her head against the footboard.

"Wait awhile," said Meridian, looking out at the burning cornfield, "and Truman and I will help you."

"You *will?*" asked Miss Treasure. Her tears, for the moment, subsided, and she smiled quite happily. Because she was so fat they had not realized how old she was, but now they could see that, indeed, she was an old woman. Her hands were ropey with veins and knotted from arthritis, her moist eyes were rimmed with cataracts. As Meridian and Truman sat with Miss Treasure on the bed, a younger woman, perhaps in her middle sixties, came to the door and leaned outward against the screen.

"Git away, Lucille!" croaked the old woman, Miss Treasure, whose voice was hoarse from crying.

"Shame," said the other woman primly, turning away. "Shame. Shame. Shame. Upon our father's name."

Miss Treasure rose from the bed and went inside the house, emerging a few minutes later with a pitcher of lemonade and a tall glossy black wig on her head. Under the wig her face was ravaged and wrinkled.

"In the first place," said Miss Treasure, sipping her lemonade, "I'm only burning what is my own. All this land you see belongs to yours truly. I can burn it up if I want to, ain't that right?"

"Sure," said Truman.

"Yes, ma'am," said Meridian.

"You hear that, sister!" called Miss Treasure.

"Humph!" came from behind the screen.

"What you say y'all name was?"

"Meridian and Truman," said Meridian.

"I'm Miss Margaret Treasure, and that's Little Sister Lucille."

"Miss Lucille Treasure," said the voice behind the screen. "I'm a Miss same as you."

"Y'all children want some lemonade?" asked Miss Treasure, pouring it.

Miss Lucille Treasure came out on the porch. Thin and the color of wet sand, she carried herself with the rigid arrogance of a walking stick held in the hand of a prince. There was cruelty in her eyes when she looked at her sister.

"What mind she got left," she sniffed, "is gone wandering."

"It ain't," protested Miss Margaret Treasure. And she began to tell her story: They had lived on the Treasure plantation—not as tenants but as owners—all their lives. How their father had managed to own a plantation in that part of Georgia they had been as children forbidden to ask. In any case, Miss Margaret Treasure—at Little Sister Lucille's prompting—had been selling bits and pieces of the place until now all that was left could be seen from the front and back porches. They had lived for years without seeing anyone, except when Little Sister Lucille went into town for staples she bought, as her father had done, twice a year.

Everything else they needed the farm provided. They had chickens, a few cows, a pig. The only time they saw people for any length of time was when Little Sister Lucille contracted with painters to come and paint the house every five years. It was at the last painting of the house that Miss Margaret Treasure's troubles started. She had fallen in love with one of the painters.

Well, Miss Margaret continued, now she was down to the last few acres and the house, which she wanted to keep. But she had to sell them in order to keep her good name and her self-respect. Because six months ago she had looked out of her bedroom window and seen a face hanging there above a ladder. It was the face of her fate. His name was Rims Mott. A dog's name, she added, bursting into fresh tears.

Little Sister Lucille stood with her hands on her hips, scowling at the quivering shoulders of her fat sister.

"They was keeping company," she said sourly, spitting over the porch rail, her brown spittle falling between two blue hydrangea bushes. "At her age! All night long I'd hear 'em at it. Yowlin' and goin' on like alley cats."

"Git back!" said the crying woman. "I don't need you to stand over me and gloat. Just because he never looked at you!"

"What do I want with a forty-five-year-old man?" asked Little Sister Lucille. "I knowed better than to let *my*self get messed up. At least," she sniffed, "I'm going to meet my maker a *clean* woman, just as pure on that day as the day I was born."

Miss Margaret's wet face was twisted in agony. From a compact which she held in trembling fingers she dabbed on more face powder, even as her tears continued to wash it away. "They say I got to marry him," she sobbed, "but I don't want to *now.*"

"Then don't marry him," said Truman and Meridian in the same breath.

"Because if I marry him," Miss Margaret continued, "he'll be sure to outlive me, and then his name will be on this house. He'll own it, and I don't trust him enough to raise no child."

Meridian's face at last showed surprise, and at the same time, the reason for Miss Margaret's tears came to Truman.

"Yes," said Little Sister Lucille smugly, watching their changed faces, "she's fat and black and seventy-two years old, and the first man she opened her legs to made her pregnant."

"Sixty-nine," said Miss Margaret.

Laughter, like a wicked silver snake, wriggled up Truman's spine. It knocked him out to hear Meridian ask, *conversationally*, "How, far along *are* you?" He glanced at her expecting to see a face fighting to control itself, but there was only a slight blush already fading into her brown skin.

"Ahhh!" Miss Margaret screamed and jumped to her feet, pulling at the heavy bed. "Help me burn it up now, y'all," she cried, and yanked with such force her wig fell off at their feet. Little Sister

Lucille grabbed it up and began to laugh, forgetting, apparently, that her own hair was severely marcelled and dyed a foolish orange.

Truman and Meridian took hold of the bed and pushed with all their strength. It hung over the edge of the porch like an ancient ship hovering over the edge of the sea. Miss Margaret pulled and the bed crashed down the steps and into the yard, Miss Margaret's leg caught under it. She did not seem to feel the pain but tugged relentlessly at the bed trying to pull it over her and out to the edge of the cornfields where the fire, by this time, had gone out.

"You're out of gasoline," said Meridian, holding up the can.

Meridian and Truman sat in the yard under a hot midsummer sun, binding Miss Margaret's leg in cold-water wraps.

"Miss Margaret," said Meridian, holding the leg on her lap and giving it an affectionate pat every now and then, "from the way you handle yourself, I don't think you're pregnant. Do you think she looks pregnant?" she asked Truman. "Truman's wife had a little girl," she explained to Miss Treasure, "so he'd be a good person to ask because he'd know."

Truman shook his head slowly, "You don't look a bit pregnant to me," he choked out.

Miss Margaret's face lit up, but quickly went dark again. "Rims said it, too," she said. "Him and Little Sister Lucille *both* said it."

"Well," said Meridian, "when we take you in to the doctor for your leg we can ask him."

Miss Margaret looked at them in fear. It had been years since she was off the plantation, and from the magazines she read the world beyond her property was not safe. She grieved over her life and moaned from the pain coming into her wounded leg. She had been a virgin until Rims came into her life, filling it with fluttery anticipation and making her body so changed, so full of hurting brightness she had known it was a sin for which she would be punished. She lay on the hot ground like a lost child, or like a dog kicked so severely it has lost its sense of smell and wanders about and leans on the tree it otherwise would have soiled.

Truman and Meridian supported her every step of the way, holding her fat arms firmly, up to the very door of the doctor's examination room. Her face, when she emerged an hour later, held a vacancy of grief that made it appear blank and smooth, as if all her wrinkles had been, by kisses, erased. The next day she came to place her name in Meridian's yellow pad.

"Ask me to do anything, young peoples," said Miss Treasure. "I'm y'all's!"

Pilgrimage

And so they must go to the prison. And so they must. And so they must see the child who murdered her child, nothing new. But the prison was. Only two stories high, it was set back from the road in a sea of green, the black trees around it like battlements around a castle. The grate of the key, the lock, the creaking door opening inward, sucking in the light into the gloom. Signing in. Hearing the harsh music of women's voices, women confined to sit and buzz like insects, whine, wait in line. Who was that person? That man/woman person with a shaved part in close-cut hair? A man's blunt face and thighs, a woman's breasts? But they had not come to stare or feel the cold security of being who they were, unconfined.

She was in a cell as small, as tidy, as a nearly empty closet. Meridian had brought magazine pictures of green fields, a blue river, a single red apple on a white page, large, containing in itself all the mystery there ever was or will be in the world. It was the apple (not the river or the green fields) the girl liked. She liked red, liked roundness, liked a clean shine on things she ate.

Yes. She had bitten her baby's cheek, bitten out a plug, before she strangled it with a piece of curtain ruffle. So round and clean it had been, too. But not red, alas, before she bit. And wasn't it right to seek to devour a perishable? That, though sweet to the nose, soft to the touch, yummy, is yet impossible to keep? It was as if (she said, dreamily) I had taken out my heart (red and round, *fine*, a glistening valentine!) and held it in my hands (my heart was sweet, sweet, smelled sweet, like apple blossoms) and took a bite out of it. It was my heart I bit, I strangled till it died. I hid beside the river. My heart the roaming dog dug up, barking for the owner of that field. My heart. Where I am (she continues) no one is. And why am I alive, without my heart? And how is this? And who, in the hell, are you?

"People who ask people to vote." (To struggle away, beyond, all in the world they have ever known.)

(She laughs, heartily and young.) Well, you don't think there's anybody here to vote? Peals of laughter washing them down to the absurdity of worms after a rain wrigglingly constructing ridges of sand to sink between before the crushing boot that's raised above comes crushing down.

"Your mother and sister told us where you were."

A mother and sister oddly smug about this child who killed her child. Thirteen (her mother said) and *too* damn grown, since before she was even ten. Doomed, I told her. Get out of my house. Walk the streets for all I care. She never was (turning to look) like Carrie Mae, the one that pained me most being born. Must have been because all my pain from Carrie Mae come then, and was got over with. Now (lifting her chin) this 'un in the prison was *too* easy coming. Like grease.

Spare me (says the girl). Across her face the sun has burned squares between the lighter color protected by the bars. I look out of my window every evening (she says) until it goes down, warming my chest. If you all can't give me back my heart (she says suddenly, with venom), go the fuck away.

It is too much for them. Outside again they are strangers to the green land, the ground they walk on, have known forever. It is so close to Meridian she takes to her sleeping bag, there to weep underneath Truman's trembling arm, there to rouse her own heart to compassion for her son. But her heart refuses to beat faster, to warm, except for the girl, the child who killed her child. Doomed, she thought, doomed. A fucking heart of stone.

Truman lay as if slaughtered, feeling a warmth, as of hot blood, wash over him. *Shame.* But for what? For whom? What had he done?

Meridian sat, watching the workmen from the city begin to clear the debris from the ditch, preparatory to filling it in (yes, the voters had won this small, vital service), and she wrote with such intensity and passion the pen dug holes in the paper—

i want to put an end to guilt
i want to put an end to shame
whatever you have done my sister
(my brother)
know i wish to forgive you
love you
it is not the crystal stone
of our innocence
that circles us
not the tooth of our purity
that bites bloody our hearts.

She slept that night with Truman's arms around her, while Truman's dreams escaped from his lips to make a moaning, crying song.

One day, after Truman—who was beginning to experience moments with Meridian when he felt intensely maternal—had wiped her forehead with a cloth soaked in cold water, Meridian wrote:

there is water in the world for us
brought by our friends
though the rock of mother and god
vanishes into sand
and we, cast out alone
to heal
and re-create
ourselves.

These poems she did not burn. She placed them just above Anne-Marion's letters, after which she did not look at the letters, the poems, or even the walls, again.

(Atonement: Later, in the Same Life)

Truman held her hands away from his shoulders. "I have something to tell you, Lynne. Try not to be upset."

"You're going to divorce me," said Lynne bravely, sillily.

"No. I don't think so. The truth is, I still love you."

"Still?"

"I always did. I love you. You irritate me sometimes . . . "

"You irritate me, often."

". . . but. But I don't desire you any more."

Lynne sank back into her rocker. Truman knelt on the floor.

"Is it because I'm fat?" she asked. "Is it because I smell, maybe? Is it because my hair is messy? Or is it because—" and she laughed a strangled laugh—"is it because I have now become Art?"

"No, no," he said, wondering about her. "I do *love you. It's just that—I don't want to do anything but provide for you and be your friend. Your brother. Can you accept that?"*

Lynne chuckled, thinking of the South, the green fields . . .

"Maybe we can start over again," she said. "Let's go back South."

"What for?*" he asked.*

Settling Accounts

"But do you know what I want from you?" Truman asked Meridian, leaning over her sleeping bag. "Promise me you won't laugh at me . . . ." He hesitated. "I want you to love me."

"But I *do* love you," said Meridian.

"You pity me. I want your love the way I had it a long time ago. I used to feel it springing out to me whenever you looked into my eyes. It flowed over me like a special sun, like grace."

"My love for you changed. . . ."

"You withdrew it."

"No, I set you free. . . ."

"Hah," he said bitterly, "why don't you admit you learned to hate me, to disrespect me, to wish I were dead. It was your contempt for me that made it impossible for me to forget."

"I meant it when I said it sets you free. You are free to be whichever way you like, to be with whoever, of whatever color or sex you like—and what you risk in being truly yourself, the way you want to be, is not the loss of me. You are *not* free, however, to think I am a fool."

He noticed, above their heads, an addition to the line of letters. A blank sheet of paper and, next to it, forming the end of the line, a photograph of an enormous bull's-eye. When he stood up close to it he discovered—after much twisting of his head and neck—that it was not a bull's-eye at all but a gigantic tree stump. A tiny branch, no larger than his finger, was growing out of one side. The piece of paper next to it was not blank, though the handwriting was grotesquely small. Even so, he recognized it as Anne-Marion's. It contained one line: "Who would be happier than you that The Sojourner did not die?" She had written, also in a minute script, "perhaps me," but then had half-erased it.

Behind him on the floor Meridian was bending forward again and again to touch her toes, her flushed face tense with determination; a rush of gratitude that she was alive flooded Truman's body. When she stopped for breath he dropped to the floor beside her and gathered her into his arms. But Meridian leaned against him for only a moment, then she continued to flex and stretch her muscles.

"Truman," Meridian said, when she lay back, exhausted, on the floor. "Do you remember what happened the last time we went out? Remember how that woman attacked me and then slammed the door in our faces?"

He remembered.

"I never explained to you why she did that. She did it because I know something about her life that she told me, but now she wishes I didn't know it because she's afraid of what people will think about her if they know. That woman left her husband because he was infatuated with his dog."

Truman laughed.

"No, no, I mean it. He was in love with a dog. He bought the best of everything for the dog to eat. He brushed its coat a dozen times a day. He talked to it constantly, ignoring his children and his wife. He let it sleep on the best bed in the guest room. Some nights he would stay with it. When his wife finally screamed and asked him why, he explained that the dog had better qualities than she had. The wife left him. Took all their five children and went to live with her mother. But her mother didn't want her because the children gave her a headache, and so she convinced the daughter that even if the story she told was true, it would be better to go back to him. Because, after all, he owned his own house and was not stingy or mean. They ate well and he did not come home drunk on the weekends and beat her. The wife had no choice; she went back to her husband because alone she could not feed her children. Of course she made her husband promise to kill the dog."

"And did he kill the dog?"

Meridian shrugged.

"I suspect that is not the point." she said.

Release

She was strong enough to go and owned nothing to pack. She had discarded her cap, and the soft wool of her newly grown hair framed her thin, resolute face. His first thought was of Lazarus, but then he tried to recall someone less passive, who had raised himself without help. Meridian would return to the world cleansed of sickness. That was what he knew.

What he *felt* was that something in her was exactly the same as she had always been and as he had, finally, succeeded in knowing her. That was the part he might now sense but could not see. He would never see "his" Meridian again. The new part had grown out of the old, though, and that was reassuring. This part of her, new, sure and ready, even eager, for the world, he knew he must meet again and recognize for its true value at some future time.

"Your ambivalence will always be deplored by people who consider themselves revolutionists, and your unorthodox behavior will cause traditionalists to gnash their teeth," said Truman, who was not, himself, concerned about either group. To him, they were practically imaginary. It was still amazing to him how deeply Meridian allowed an idea—no matter where it came from—to penetrate her life.

"I hate to think of you always alone."

"But that is my value," said Meridian. "Besides, all the people who are as alone as I am will one day gather at the river. We will watch the evening sun go down. And in the darkness maybe we will know the truth."

She hugged him, long, lingeringly (her nose and lips rooting about at his neck, causing him to laugh), and then she went, walking as if hurrying to catch up with someone.

Truman turned, tears burning his face, and began, almost blindly, to read the poems she had left on the walls. He could not bring himself to read the letters yet. It was his house now, after all. His cell. Tomorrow the people would come and bring him food. Someone would come and milk his cow. They would wait patiently for him to perform, to take them along the next guideless step. Perhaps he would.

"whatever you have done, my brother . . . know i wish to forgive you . . . love you   it is not the crystal stone of our innocence   that circles us   not the tooth of our purity   that bites bloody our hearts."

Truman felt the room begin to turn and fell to the floor. A moment later, dizzy, he climbed shakily into Meridian's sleeping bag. Underneath his cheek he felt the hard edge of her cap's visor, he pulled it out and put it on his head. He had a vision of Anne-Marion herself arriving, lost, someday, at the door, which would remain open, and wondered if Meridian knew that the sentence of bearing the conflict in her own soul which she had imposed on herself—and lived through—must now be borne in terror by all the rest of them.

Large print edition design by Terri Wright
Cover by Jody Chapel, Cover to Cover Design,
Denver, Colorado
Composed in 16/18 pt. Plantin by QuadraType,
San Francisco, California
Printing and binding by Braun-Brumfield, Inc.,
Ann Arbor, Michigan